MOLLY
& PIM
and the
Millions of
Stars

Also by Martine Murray

MOLLY & PIM

and the Millions of Stars

Martine Murray

Alfred A. Knopf 🐎 New York

Text copyright © 2015 by Martine Murray
Jacket art copyright © 2017 by Jessica Allen
Interior illustrations copyright © 2015 by Martine Murray

Visit us on the Web! randomhousekids.com

Educators and librarians, for a variety of teaching tools, visit us at RHTeachersLibrarians.com

Library of Congress Cataloging-in-Publication Data
Names: Murray, Martine, author.
Title: Molly and Pim and the millions of stars / Martine Murray.
Description: First American edition. | New York : Alfred A. Knopf, 2017.
| "2015" | "Originally published in paperback by The Text Publishing Company, Melbourne, Australia in 2015"—Copyright page. |
Summary: Molly longs for normalcy but when her mother accidentally turns herself into a tree, Molly must embrace all the things she has tried to run away from.
Identifiers: LCCN 2015034847 | ISBN 978-0-399-55040-9 (trade) | ISBN 978-0-399-55043-0 (pbk.) | ISBN 978-0-399-55041-6 (lib. bdg.) | ISBN 978-0-399-55042-3 (ebook)
Subjects: | CYAC: Mothers—Fiction. | Friendship—Fiction. | Self-acceptance—Fiction. | Magic—Fiction. | Australia—Fiction.
Classification: LCC PZ7.M9637 Mo 2017 | DDC [Fic]—dc23

The text of this book is set in 12-point Caslon 540.

Printed in the United States of America
January 2017
10 9 8 7 6 5 4 3 2 1

First American Edition

Random House Children's Books supports the First Amendment and celebrates the right to read.

WARNING, WARNING, WARNING

Don't attempt to make any herb potions, even though this book may inspire such activities, unless someone in the know has made sure each plant is the right plant and not a sneaky poisonous one.

To Little Pump and all the kids
who have lived in our garden:
Joey, Jip, Miro, Ollie, Pearl, Zoe,
Owen, Matilda, Sally, Sesi

And in loving memory of Oshi,
the brightest star

Amaranth

CHAPTER I

A PRICKLY DAY

W hen Molly woke up, she could tell it was one of those days. She sniffed to make sure. Then she sat up straight and called out in her most thunderous voice, "Hey, I'm awake."

Just as she suspected, there was no answer. The house hardly creaked. The Gentleman didn't even crow. On a day like this, when the morning was making white, shimmery patterns on her wall and the birds' singing was sun-drenched and giddy, her mama would already be gone into the woods.

Molly was the only girl whose mama went into the woods, and Molly didn't like it. She turned over in her bed and thought: I just won't get up at all, today is a prickly day.

A day arrives with a certain feeling about it, and this one was a brimming and giving-forth day, a day when the wild herbs would be just right for collecting. The vibration in them was the best at dawn. Molly didn't like to think about plants vibrating or emitting or sensing, as this was all part of the strangeness of things, and she objected strongly to strangeness and tried to pretend it wasn't there.

Yet something had woken her; something had let her know today had arrived with its own prickly plans. She suspected it was vibrations. Terrible, secret, mysterious, and uninvited vibrations.

Molly blocked her ears with her hands and imagined that her mama was just like Ellen's mother, who drove a nice clean car and gave Ellen muesli bars in plastic wrappers and let her watch whatever she liked on television. Molly flexed her toes to let them know she would soon be depending on them. Everything was bound to be in a contrary way this morning; even her toes might misbehave. At least, she comforted herself, at least while her mama was gone, she could eat crumpets from the packet, with blackberry jam. Molly liked things that came in packets. Packets were what Ellen's mother had.

At this happy thought, Molly sat up again and called to Claudine the cat, but Claudine didn't come. Claudine never came when she was called. Molly found her curled up like a croissant on the piano. Claudine was fat and black and glossy with white paws, one of which she glamorously extended beyond her nose. She glanced at Molly and appeared to be thinking lofty, superior thoughts about Molly in her mismatched pajamas: spotty on top and stripy on the bottom. Molly's mama would say, "Claudine thinks we are slobs!" Claudine was not French, but it was as if she thought she was. It was as if she should have been fed *tarte aux pommes* (which is French for "apple tart") all day long.

"Well," said Molly, climbing onto the stool so she could stroke Claudine's nice fat tummy, "no one really loves you, Claudine, anyway. We just tolerate you." Then she spelled out the word, t-o-l-e-r-a-t-e, as if this might help Claudine understand. But Claudine, as usual, didn't care about words or love. She only raised her head to look around the room for sunny spots, and then, finding none better than where she was, she closed her eyes again.

Molly spread butter and blackberry jam onto two

crumpets and squished the jam into the holes so she could put even more on top. Balancing the plate on her hand above her head, she danced an Egyptian dance of the seven veils at Claudine. Claudine ignored the dancing, so Molly put down her plate and picked up her ukulele and sang "The Drunken Sailor" very loudly until Claudine stood up, arched her tail stiffly, and slunk out into the kitchen.

Molly went back to bed with her crumpets and ate them by herself. Once they were gone, she let herself feel sorry for Claudine. It was a shame that she didn't appreciate Egyptian dances and nice old folk songs, or get to eat crumpets. Molly went and fetched Claudine and plonked her on the pillow so she could lick away the crumbs and blobs of dripped jam. This way her mama wouldn't notice that she'd eaten crumpets in bed.

Claudine stood and licked in an elegant fashion. She was quite partial to blackberry jam. It must be what cats eat in Paris, thought Molly as she pulled on her boots. Then she marched outside to let out the Gentleman and the chickens and set off toward the woods to find her mama.

The woods were not far, just over a bridge and a little way up the dirt road. The deeper Molly went into the woods, the thicker and darker they became. The tops of the trees crowded the sky and let the light filter down and spread in patches on the ground. Molly was not scared of the woods with their moments of darkness—she had followed her mama in there lots of times.

The birds were noisy, and Molly felt sure that if she listened well enough, they would tell her where her mama was. But Molly also knew that if she kept stomping along, her mama would find her, as her mama was always quiet and watchful and listening, almost as if she was a creature herself.

Sure enough, it wasn't long before her mama appeared, landing silently on the path. With her was Maude the dog, a black-and-white collie with slightly too-large, black, hairy ears and a freckled nose. Maude dropped a stick at Molly's feet. Molly picked it up and threw it, and Maude dashed off after it. She was so easily pleased.

Molly's mama smiled and pulled off her straw hat with the red ribbon. A patch of sun made her mad curly hair shine like a halo. Her legs and feet were bare except for her scuffed white sneakers, and she wore an old, faded sundress with a cardigan. She wound her hair up and stuck a wooden pin in it and bent down to kiss Molly's cheek.

"Molly," she sighed, "you're not even dressed. You're wearing pajamas."

"And you're not even at home," declared Molly. "And I'm meant to be at school."

Her mama smiled. She was not fussed about school. "Really? Is it already that time? I was distracted. Did Claudine show you the note I left? I made you a fruit salad." She put down her basket of herbs, and Molly peered into it. Miner's lettuce, purslane, rose hips, and saltbush berries.

There was a time when Molly had known a lot about herbs, but she had recently decided not to know anything about them at all.

"Claudine didn't even say good morning. I had to make crumpets."

Molly could tell her mama's thoughts were else-where. She hardly seemed to register that Molly had eaten crumpets instead of fruit salad.

Molly tugged at her mama's hand as they walked along the track. Her mama looked at her, with surprise. It always surprised her when Molly noticed things. In fact, most things surprised her: it was as if she never suspected anything would happen, but things always did. She pulled her cardigan close.

"It's the neighbors," her mama said with a shudder. "They're complaining again."

The neighbors were staunch, zipped-up, sneering people who glanced away when you went near them, but were always peering over fences and squinting into everyone else's lives. They despised unruly back gardens with dogs or birds or noisy children, and they had appointed themselves the neighborhood watchdogs of all things overgrown, out of bounds, or against the rules. Their house was a grim brick house with a pebble-mix garden, in which sat a white turtle made of clay. There was a flagpole in the front, and on certain days they raised the nation's flag. It made Molly feel mutinous every time she saw it.

Prudence Grimshaw had a long, narrow head and short, colorless hair, which rose upward and hovered above two stabbing eyes and a short line of lip. Ernest Grimshaw was rarely seen, though when you did see him, mostly all you noticed was a very prominent chin and an even more prominent stomach, which thrust him forward at a determined pace toward his large black car, whose doors he slammed with gusto.

On a day like today, complainers complained even more loudly. They complained all over the blue sky. Life's quiet hum rattled them because they couldn't hear it, but they sensed it in others, they sensed it in Molly's mother, and they shouted it down. As far as Molly could tell, the only thing the Grimshaws liked was each other, and Molly found that endlessly perplexing, as they were the most unlikable people Molly had ever met.

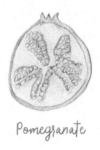

Pomegranate

CHAPTER 2
ELLEN AND PIM

"You were late again, Molly," Ellen Palmer said at recess.

Molly didn't like the way Ellen stated the obvious, but she was prepared to overlook it because Ellen Palmer was her best friend, her always-there, dependable best friend. Also, Ellen had an enviably normal life, and Molly believed that if she stayed close to Ellen Palmer's normal life, it might rub off on her. Molly tried hard to hide all the not-quite-normal parts of her own life. Having a mama, for instance, who had no respect for the rules that others lived by and who appeared to be always muddled and dreaming and in the midst of many projects, which included poetry, fermentation, and animal rescue, and who went collecting wild herbs at dawn was something Molly thought best kept to herself.

Molly glanced at Ellen's morning snack. It was in a packet. An apricot muesli bar. Molly had a pomegranate. She chewed resentfully at the dark pink pips. What she wanted most of all was not to stand out one bit.

Ellen had plaits and a mother who helped out at craft class and a father who could fix shelves and a brother with a football. And they all lived in a red-brick house with a dishwasher and a trampoline. Molly's house might look like a normal house from the outside, but on the inside it was quite different. As soon as you walked in, instead of a pleasantly regular feeling, there was an airy, open space with not one proper corner or straight line. Scatterings of large, brightly patterned cushions, Persian carpets, billowy curtains, and low-lying beds covered in sequined rugs made the room feel like a Gypsy caravan. The walls were lined with shelves of books, bottles, candles, little statues, carvings, potted plants, and trinkets from faraway places. Molly's older twin brothers had moved out of the house, first into an old caravan in the garden, and then they had gone farther, to faraway places with exciting names like Morocco, Madagascar, and, lately, Cuba. Most older brothers got normal jobs. Freya Mitchum's older brother worked at the pie shop. But he was grumpy and had turned pudding-like in his body.

"I slept in," Molly declared, and blew a pip out of her mouth toward the sandpit, only it didn't make it that far. It landed quite near Ellen's foot in its brand-new lime-green sandal. Ellen squished it with her toe.

"What's that?" she said. "It looks weird."

"Pomegranate," said Molly.

Ellen showed no further interest in the pomegranate and twirled her lime-green sandal admiringly.

"The Egyptians buried their dead with pomegranates," Molly elaborated. Sometimes Molly was disappointed by Ellen's lack of interest in interesting things. She stood up quickly and pointed at Pim Wilder, who was the oddest boy in the school.

Pim was bent in a suspicious way over the school vegetable patch, as if he was talking to the silver beet. Pim Wilder was always worth watching. He was either up to something or getting in trouble for something. And if he was getting in trouble, he never showed any shame. Instead, a smile played across his eyes. Rules just seemed to limit him. It was as if he could hardly bring himself even to consider them, let alone obey them. But facts about the world sprang him to life. In class he offered up the strangest sorts of knowledge—about birds, planets, outer space, music. He once told them of the now-extinct elephant bird of Madagascar, which laid an egg that weighed as much as a small child. And a homing pigeon in World War II who lost an eye and a leg while carrying a message, then won a medal and had its leg replaced with a wooden one. He said that Earth is the only planet not named after a god, and that each winter about one septillion snow crystals drop from the sky.

"What's a septillion, anyway?" sniggered Bruce Layne.

"A trillion trillions," replied Pim.

Bruce Layne sniggered again, because he had to hide the fact that he didn't know what a trillion was either.

Pim Wilder wasn't talking to the vegetables. He had pulled off a seed head and was examining it in the palm of his hand.

Molly was secretly fascinated by Pim Wilder. He didn't move with the pack. He wasn't drawn by the cool talk and the latest fads. And this made him interesting, and a little intimidating too. Ellen was afraid of him. But Ellen was easily afraid. She would never walk in the woods on her own or rescue a spider from the bath. If Molly told Ellen about her mama's herbs and potions, Ellen might even find this too strange and scary. Molly never told anyone about her mama's potions. Already, everyone thought it was funny that her mama rode a yellow bike with two seats, one for Molly, and that when it rained, she fastened umbrellas to the handlebars. Pim Wilder would probably love her mama's bike.

As if he heard her thinking, Pim turned toward them. Ellen clutched at Molly's hand as he walked over, with his shoulders happily bunched upward. He was brimming with a secret joy.

"I'll tell you something," he said. "When you see the seeds of a plant, you see something that's been there since the Roman times. The Romans had those same seeds growing. That's historical. That's like . . ." He trailed off and turned his face to the sky, as if he might see something there, something historical. But perhaps he saw something else, because, without even a beat or a nod, he walked away.

Ellen shook her head. "He's strange."

Molly nodded. Even though Ellen found a lot of things strange, it was important to agree. Because Molly liked Ellen. Because Ellen wasn't a sniggerer, and she wasn't a boaster either. Molly had been best friends with Ellen from the very start of school, when Ellen had wept because a frog got cut in half in the sandpit by Toby Nottingham's spade. Ellen could sing like a canary, and often you could hear her coming because of the little song that floated ahead of her. Her world was like a nest, comfortable and safe and just her size. And Ellen was like a little bird, in fact. Molly did always like those little birds the best in her own garden. The littlest birds sang the nicest songs.

But Pim, with his outer-space dreams, was way too big to make sense to Ellen.

If Molly was going to be a part of Ellen Palmer's world of songs and pop stars—that glorious, up-front world that trembled with starlike explosions in pink, in plastic, in homely razzle-dazzle—then it was important that no one knew she was curious about Pim Wilder.

The Gentleman

⤜❧ CHAPTER 3 ❧⤛
ERNEST GRIMSHAW

Molly's mama was only slightly different from other mothers, but in Molly's eyes she was very obviously different. When school was over and everyone poured out of their classrooms, the other mothers gathered in groups and chatted, but Molly's mama stood alone in the shade of the buddleia bush. She looked to Molly like an owl, wide-eyed and wary, and so relieved to see Molly that she glided out of the bush as if the task of gathering Molly up and steering her home suddenly gave her the right weight in the world.

Molly and her mama rode home on the yellow bike.

They always got off at the bottom of the hill and walked up to their house at the top. It sat beside a cluster of old pine trees that leaned dangerously and was home to a flock of cockatoos who flew shrieking into the trees, like white handkerchiefs toppling out of the blue sky.

As Molly and her mama walked up the hill, a large man came thundering toward them like a boulder rolling downhill, gathering speed as he neared them. His body pitched forward, his elbows flapped, and his hands bundled into fists and pummeled the air. Molly could tell that, like all big boulders, he meant to have an impact.

"Oi," he shouted. The word seemed to fly out of him like a bullet. And then in a fury of panting, he miraculously ground to a halt in front of them. His face was red and gleaming with sweat, which he swiped at savagely with his forearm.

It was Ernest Grimshaw, squinting and sneering and puffing all at once.

"Hello," said Molly's mama.

"I went up to your house now, but you weren't there," Ernest Grimshaw accused, waving his finger toward the house as if they needed to be reminded where they lived.

Molly's mama stared at him, a little amused. Then she remembered her manners and replied, "We're on our way home now, Mr. Grimshaw. Is there something you wanted?" Next to the blustering, accusing, over-heated boulder of a man, Molly's mama seemed like a wisp of grass, straight and calm in the sun.

"I came to tell you to get rid of that blasted rooster. It keeps waking us up at dawn with its crowing. And if you don't get rid of it, well, I warn you"—he gave a violent snort—"I'll take an ax to it myself!" He shook his fists, as if he held the handle of the ax right then, and Molly's mama ducked to avoid being struck.

Molly let go of the bike and stepped forward. "You can't kill our rooster. He is a gentleman. That's his name: the Gentleman. He's sweet enough you can pick him up and cuddle him. So we won't be letting him get the ax from you."

Ernest Grimshaw's mouth fell open. His little round eyes flared as if they were about to pop out of his head.

Molly's mama clasped Molly to her side and glanced at her with a look of tenderness. "Mr. Grim-shaw, how about we try to find some arrangement so that the Gentleman doesn't wake you? You know, I actually find that after time the sound of crowing can become quite soothing and familiar and almost as golden as the dawn, and then it just seeps like a little song into my dreams. . . ."

"What?" the man roared. A wind of hot breath grazed Molly's face. "Are you mad? A little song? Crowing is crowing. Nothing musical about it. And I don't care if he's got a name or not. He could be Mozart for all I care."

He turned as if this was the final word. But then he swiveled around and thrust his fat finger at Molly. "And tell her, tell that little upstart, she needs to show some respect for her elders. Or she'll have something coming at her too." Ernest Grimshaw nodded in agreement with himself.

Molly drew herself up indignantly to reply, but her mama held her back. And they watched as the barrel-like form of Ernest Grimshaw turned and marched toward his own house.

Molly's mama whistled. "That poor man. How awful it must be to be him. I think you and I need an ice cream. And, while I think about it, do stay out of his way, won't you? No point aggravating angry people. At least until I sort out this business with the Gentleman."

Molly nodded, but only to please her mama. She had no intention of staying out of Ernest Grimshaw's way if he came threatening the Gentleman.

Castor Oil Plant

Chapter 4

PRUDENCE GRIMSHAW

Molly and her mama ate homemade banana ice cream on the seesaw. Molly's mama liked to stand in the middle and tip it up and down. Molly sat on the edge and dangled her feet.

Sounds of banging from the Grimshaws' house floated up toward them, but otherwise the world seemed to disappear, or at least to tilt away. Wafts of summer smells, squished grass and lavender, drifted over them.

Molly puzzled over what Pim Wilder had said about seeds continuing on forever. Perhaps he was marveling at how one small seed dropped on the ground, with only sun and water added, becomes a huge tree. This wasn't something Molly had ever thought about, but Pim was right: a tiny seed contained the whole magic of a towering tree. Molly was about to point this out to her mama when a shrill, piercing voice rang out across the garden. Maude leaped up with a short, appalled bark.

Prudence Grimshaw's head poked over the fence. "I'll have you know that if it was you, you will be punished. We have called the police!"

There, thought Molly, there was nothing more prickly than that. She had been right about the vibrations. Molly and her mama both stared at Prudence Grimshaw in confusion. Prudence Grimshaw held a hammer in one hand and she gripped the fence with the other, while nosing the air as if sniffing for clues. Her eyes bore down on them accusingly.

"What are you talking about, Mrs. Grimshaw?" said Molly's mama.

"I'm talking about our turtle. Someone stole it." She gave the hammer a little jerk and looked over her nose at them with a suspicious stare; her voice was suddenly measured and low. "And whoever took it thought it was funny to leave a watermelon in its place."

Molly smothered a giggle.

"Do you think that's funny?" Prudence Grimshaw shrieked. "Because you won't when we find out who did it."

"It wasn't me," said Molly flatly. "I don't like pretend turtles."

"We hope you find it, Mrs. Grimshaw. It was probably just a joke and the turtle will be returned," said Molly's mama with a weary sigh.

Mrs. Grimshaw made a horsey sort of harrumph and disappeared. The sounds of banging recommenced.

This time Molly sighed. "Mama, she is more noisy than the Gentleman and Maude put together, and one hundred times nastier too. Let's move our house to the other side of the pines."

Molly's mama laughed. "Houses are much too stubborn to be moved."

Molly knew what her mama would be thinking. She would be thinking of other solutions, weird ones. "Mama," she cautioned, "this isn't a time for potions. You can't stop nastiness in neighbors with a potion."

"We have to look at it another way, Molly," her mama replied. "What we have is a musical problem. We have to resolve it into a new sort of harmony."

Molly squinted into the sun. She wanted her mama

to be like Ellen Palmer's mother, and to have apricot muesli bars put in her lunch box. Molly couldn't even imagine what Ellen Palmer's mother would do in this situation. But she knew that Ellen Palmer's mother would not be thinking of a musical solution.

"I have an idea," said her mama.

Oh no, thought Molly.

"We'll grow a tree. That way we'll have something beautiful to look at and the Grimshaws won't see in when they poke their heads over the fence. That will be our new harmony. A very beautiful large tree. Perhaps a white cedar with the lilac blossom. Or a weeping myrtle. What do you think? Even an oak . . ."

"But, Mama, trees take a long time to grow." Molly thought again of the seed in the ground.

"Yes, usually, but I think I can make it grow very quickly."

Molly said nothing. She stared gravely at the sky.

"We could get an acorn from that glorious tree in the gardens. The huge, spreading one near the playground. I'll soak the acorn in a special decoction. And then, when we plant it, it should grow in a week."

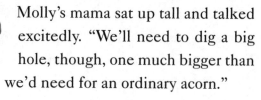

Molly's mama sat up tall and talked excitedly. "We'll need to dig a big hole, though, one much bigger than we'd need for an ordinary acorn."

"You hate digging, Mama. It makes your back ache."

Though this was true, her mama ignored it. She jumped off the seesaw, waving her hand in the air. "Well, I can still dig it."

Digging holes made them both think of Molly's father, as her mama always famously claimed that digging holes was the most useful thing he'd ever done around the house.

Molly's father was an adventurer and had disappeared somewhere in the Sierra Maestra, a mountain range in Cuba. Molly's twin brothers had both gone to Cuba to look for him. Miro, however, had joined a mariachi band with his trumpet and bought a silver caravan, while Yip had met a peasant girl called Olga who lived in a hut in the mountains and who persuaded him to take her to Mexico, where she modeled bathing suits for a magazine.

Molly could barely remember her father. There was a photo of him stuck on the fridge with a frog magnet: a broad-shouldered and slightly podgy twenty-nine-year-old man, smoking and squinting, with his thumb tucked in his pants.

Molly would always remember when he left, though. She had cried until she felt so tired she couldn't cry anymore, and then she lay quite still for as long as a week, as quiet and dazed as a little mouse. Her mama gave her herbal concoctions and wrapped her up and told her stories and slowly coaxed her back.

Molly had decided not to think about her dad again and never, never to cry again. And she never had.

She could be very strong about some things.

Mandrake

CHAPTER 5

AN ANGEL

While lining up outside the school hall for assembly the next day, Molly tugged on Ellen's hand and whispered, "Mama and I have a problem. We officially have the world's nastiest neighbors. Ernest Grimshaw looks like a large puffer fish and he wants to kill the Gentleman with an ax. And his wife thinks we stole her fake turtle, and they're constantly shouting things over the fence. Mama thinks we should grow a tree and block them out."

Ellen's nose twitched like a rabbit's. "That's silly. It will take forever."

Molly didn't want to tell Ellen that her mama

intended to use a potion to make it grow fast. She wished Ellen hadn't said it was silly, though.

"I think we should move the house," Molly said.

"But you can't just move a house." Ellen shrugged. She did think about things in a relentlessly practical way.

Molly began to regret starting the conversation. Weren't best friends supposed to be understanding? Weren't you supposed to tell them something if it was on your mind? But telling Ellen made the situation seem hopeless.

"Nothing is impossible, just hard," said Molly, plucking a piece of buddleia and pressing it soothingly under her nose. "If the Egyptians built pyramids by hand, surely we can move a house?"

Ellen frowned. "Easier to just ignore the neighbors, I reckon. How old are they? Maybe they'll soon be shoved off to a retirement home anyway."

Molly gave a limp nod. "I guess so." She didn't believe it, though. No one was shoving those Grimshaws anywhere.

After assembly, a strange thing happened. Hoisted up alongside the flag was a papier-mâché angel, with peach pits for eyes and yellow-tipped cockatoo feathers on its wings. No one usually noticed the flag, but everyone noticed the angel. And the angel seemed to know it was much more remarkable than an old flag. The kids laughed. The teachers frowned, except for the art teacher, who hid her grin behind her hand. Who had put it there?

Sinclair Jones threw a plum at it, but it missed. Molly and Ellen watched the commotion from beneath the loquat tree. A competition had sprung up as a result of Sinclair Jones's plum. Kids threw shoes, tennis balls, stones, and seedpods, and one of the older boys even tried a can of baked beans, which missed, but smashed on the ground, spilling its guts very satisfyingly. The happy shouts caused Miss Ward to come clucking and calling for a stop to the game.

Though it had taken a hit or two, the angel held fast.

Molly watched Pim Wilder, who hadn't joined in on the throwing, but then again Pim rarely joined in. He sat on a low brick wall, leaning back, arms crossed, with the usual dark gleam in his eyes and a small, mysterious case slung over his shoulder.

"Bet I know who made that angel," said Molly, aiming her gaze directly at Pim Wilder.

Ellen looked over at him and nodded. "But why do you think he made it and how did he get it up there?"

Molly shrugged. "Who knows? Maybe it's like a

sort of talisman, something that brings you good luck or wards off evil spirits."

"Do you believe in that kind of thing?" Ellen tossed her plaits behind her shoulders one at a time. Molly rubbed at her own hair, which was short, dark, and curly and wouldn't go into plaits, as it was too disobedient. But she couldn't quite find a finished sort of answer.

"Well, I don't believe, but I don't not believe either. And I like not knowing better than knowing."

Before Ellen could decide whether she agreed or not, Pim Wilder got up off the wall and glided, as if drawn by other forces, to the base of the flagpole. Molly and Ellen watched him. Pim was tall and he usually moved in fits and starts. When he walked or ran, his arms and legs were flung forward, as if he wasn't sure of the length of his own limbs. But now he moved without one fit or start, more as if he was in a royal procession, and, once arrived, he stood quite still. He craned his head upward and took a camera out of the case. He lifted it to his eye. It was an old-fashioned type of camera that needed focusing, and as he took the photo, he looked as if he knew exactly what he was doing.

Either he hadn't even noticed that Molly and Ellen were still there, or he didn't care.

Acorn

CHAPTER 6

FEELINGS THAT CREEP AND SKITTER

Molly found it hard to concentrate at school. At home, her mama was building a dark, boxlike bedroom for the Gentleman, with curtained windows, so that he wouldn't notice the dawn arriving and wouldn't crow till they let him out, after Mr. Grimshaw was awake. Maybe her mama would focus on that and forget about her potions and the fast-growing oak tree. Molly was worried about this witchy interference, and now that she felt Ellen didn't understand her worries, she had to keep them locked up inside her head.

Molly's mama was waiting for her after school.

She was flushed with excitement and a plan that they would ride home via the gardens so they could hunt for the right acorn for the tree-growing potion. Molly's hopes fell. Not only had her mama remembered, but she also wanted to drag Molly along with her. The last thing Molly wanted was to be seen with her mama in the gardens examining acorns.

"Can't I just go home and you go on your own?" she pleaded.

Her mama tilted her head and gave Molly a look of curious concern. "You don't have to come if you don't want to," she said softly, sweeping an unruly lock of hair from her eyes. Then she smiled at Molly.

Molly sometimes suspected her mama's gentle smiles radiated their own magic, as Molly instantly felt that she should go. She heaved a big, grouchy sigh. "Okay, I'll come, but I'm not looking at acorns; I'll just wait while you do it."

The gardens were large, with avenues of oaks and elms all the way around the outside. There was a small lake and a few flower beds, but mostly it was a sprawling lawn of all sorts of trees. The largest of all was a towering English oak, which had been planted by a duke more than a hundred years ago.

It was to that tree that Molly and her mama headed.

They had just got off the bike to push it over the grass when Molly noticed Pim Wilder. He was squatting at the base of a large tree, examining something. He frowned slightly, but his eyes were bright, and he stared at the thing in his hand with such intensity that Molly wanted to run over to see what it was. But she also wanted to hurry past in case he saw her and asked what she was doing there with her odd mama on a yellow bike.

Molly watched as Pim prodded and pushed the thing with his fingers and then stood up and stared into the leafy canopy of the tree. He was still holding what seemed to be a ball of dirt in his open palm. Molly craned her neck to look closer, and Pim Wilder suddenly turned around. He stared straight at her. She quickly looked away, but his eye had caught hers.

Pim looked at Molly without the least bit of surprise or interest. Then he lifted his head in a slight gesture of recognition, and a flicker of amusement passed across his eyes. Molly blushed as she pushed the bike onward.

She was perplexed. She hadn't wanted Pim to see

her, as his manner was unusual. But to have him notice her and show no interest had embarrassed her. The truth was that she found Pim interesting. Molly didn't like to admit this, even to herself, but now it seemed well and truly proven, not only to Molly but to Pim as well.

But why wasn't Molly interesting to him? He probably thought she was only interested in girlish things, which wasn't true. She stomped ahead, way past Pim. In her head, she began to compose a list of all the very great things she was interested in. Tree houses, for one. She liked dogs too. And songs. And table tennis. Trampolines and stilts and handstands. Caravans. And anything mysterious. These were worthy things. Pim had got her wrong.

Molly watched her mama picking up acorns and examining them. The funny thing was, there was something about her mama's complete absorption in the task that was exactly like the way Pim had been at the base of his tree. Molly shook her head. This was all very confusing.

She called out to her mama, "Can we go now? I'm hungry."

Her mama looked up with surprise and then

grinned. "Of course. I think I've found the one I need."

Molly didn't want to ask how her mama could tell one acorn from another, because she knew the answer would be something she didn't want to hear. So they got on their bike and rode along the gravel path all the way home. Neither of them spoke. Molly's mama hummed as she rode, busily thinking out her new potion. Molly was wondering about Pim Wilder and his mysterious ball of dirt.

That night Molly's mama stayed up all night, reading her books on plants, scribbling notes and making drawings in her red notebook, pounding leaves and roots, extracting drops of plant essence, and dropping them onto copper chloride plates of crystallized salts, boiling others, or soaking them in vodka. She was making a potion stronger than any she had ever made before.

Molly woke in the night to see her mama completely entranced by her work, bent over the small wooden desk with a determined frown on her face. She lifted the dark bottles and vials and droppers, fell to her knees to rummage through the baskets of dried plants and seeds and roots, and flipped vigorously through her books on the uses of herbs and weeds.

Molly sighed and rolled over. The activity of her mama's thinking was like a strange, insistent wind rustling through the dark night, seeping into her body and making her turn and twist and anticipate something. What is about to happen, and why do I feel it's big? she wondered.

It's just what happens, she reassured herself, when Mama starts making potions. You wake up in the night and you get feelings. Feelings that creep and skitter within you like a frightened mouse darting for the corners and holes, feelings that never quite announce themselves either.

And with that thought, Molly fell back to sleep.

Borage

CHAPTER 7

BORAGE TEA

When Molly woke up, her mama was still working. She moved slowly now. She rubbed at her eyes and leaned, swaying and blinking, into the light. She looked as if she might fall asleep and fold down in a small, disheveled pile on the floor.

"Mama, did you stay up all night? You need to go and sleep." Molly stuck her hands on her hips.

Her mama smiled faintly and sank down into the chair.

"All I need is a cup of borage tea. We've got a tree to plant today." She picked up a jar and pointed to the acorn inside a brown liquid.

It was Saturday. The house was bathed in the scents of lemon and rosemary oil, which had burned all through the night. Maude lay in her basket, one large black ear cocked in case there was movement. Claudine had taken advantage of Mama's empty bed and lay curled up and sunken into the yellow quilt. The sky outside looked bright and promising, and everything was quiet at the Grimshaws'.

Possibly everything could be all right after all, thought Molly. But possibly everything will go wrong too, she thought as well. It was her habit to think one thing and then the exact opposite. What would it be like to be Ellen Palmer this morning? Or what would it be like to be Pim Wilder? She knew what Ellen would be doing, but what about Pim? She couldn't imagine what he did when he wasn't at school. Look at things through telescopes? Map the stars? Make papier-mâché angels? Molly knew that Ellen would be on her way to pony club. With her camel-colored jodhpurs and her hair in neat plaits, Ellen wouldn't have to worry that her mama had stayed up all night long.

"No," said Molly, accidentally out loud.

"No?" repeated her mama vaguely. "Oh, you're right, the hole. I'll dig it now." She stood up, rubbing at her back and reaching for her straw hat.

"I'll dig the hole," Molly offered politely.

"No, you make the borage tea."

Molly was relieved, but she felt a little guilty for not sharing in her mama's eagerness to plant the tree. She glanced warily at the acorn in its potion. It looked as if it had sunk to the bottom of a dirty pond. Molly couldn't see anything magical about it. She sniffed the wet, earthy, sharp smell, which was exactly as you would expect rotting leaves in winter to smell. It was probably just a normal old acorn, Molly scoffed to herself.

She rummaged through the washing basket, found her favorite red dress, put it on, and ran outside with Maude to get some borage. Borage was growing everywhere in the garden, even where it was not meant to be. It had large, squishy, slightly prickly leaves and tiny blue flowers. Molly picked a bunch, plucking off the flowers and eating them as she went. She shooed the chickens and picked up the Gentleman, who was most handsome with his white feathers and glorious red comb. She swished at the harlequin beetles that were eating the cherry tomatoes, and picked some basil, because her mama often liked basil and borage together.

Molly ran inside and boiled the water and steeped

the herbs in the teapot. Then she took the pot and a cup outside to where her mama was digging the hole.

Her mama stood up and rubbed her back and tore off her gloves. The wide brim of her straw hat sagged, but Molly could see her cheeks were red.

"It seems such a big hole for an acorn, but the roots will need lots of room to grow quickly. Ah, tea . . . thank you."

"Borage and basil," Molly declared.

Her mama smiled, but she seemed too tired to be impressed. They both sat there and watched a willie wagtail dance in the mottled shade under the lilly pilly tree.

Molly poured the tea. Maude nuzzled up to Mama, who lazily gave her a pat.

Mama sipped her tea, peeping over the teacup at Molly. "The hole is almost deep enough, and I think we might see something happen as soon as we plant the acorn," she said as she put down the cup.

Everything felt so sleepy and lazy and sunny that it seemed impossible for it all to change as violently as it did in the very next instant.

Molly's mama took her jar of potion and held it up to the light and shook it gently. The acorn jiggled inside the jar. She drank another mouthful of tea. She leaned back and sighed, closed her eyes, and let the sun fall on her face. Then she raised her hand to her mouth and drank again. She gulped. Her eyes widened. She stared in horror at what she held in her hand.

It was the jar of acorn potion.

Molly stared too. Something terrible was happening. "Mama?" she breathed.

But it seemed that her mama couldn't talk. Her eyes closed and she wobbled, but instead of falling over, she began to turn a dark, muddy color. Her body welled up and up and grew tall, and her arms shot outward, as rigid as a scarecrow's. A loud creaking and splitting sound came from her body, and her eyes were wide, as if something had tugged suddenly at her eyelids. She stared at Molly with a look of great yearning. Then her eyes swept shut and she seemed to be sucked inward as her breath blew out of her in a violent blast.

Maude began to run in circles.

Molly froze. Her mama's body turned into a trunk. Her skin turned to bark. Her arms became branches. And her face vanished in the crown of leaves that spread across the summer sky. All that remained was her straw hat, which hung perilously from a branch high up in the tree, its thin red ribbon flying gaily in the wind.

Molly's heart was very loud inside her. Her eyes were stuck wide open, and her legs began to tremble. She crouched down and put her hands on the warm grass. Then she crawled toward the tree that was her mama and put her head against it.

She squeezed her eyes very tightly shut and told herself she mustn't cry.

Lemon Balm Tea

CHAPTER 8
CHOCOLATE-AND-CASHEW BALLS

Even for the bravest of the brave, it is a terrible shock to watch your mama turn into a tree. Molly crouched down and rocked herself gently. She drew herself into a ball, like a bug, and squeezed herself hard, trying not to let anything come in or go out. Her thoughts raced around and around.

Her mama was gone.

Her mama was a tree.

It was a sunny Saturday morning, and half the town was already up and bustling about, and the hum of activity crept up from the valley. But Molly stayed curled up by the tree. Maude lay beside her, and

Claudine had leaped off the fence to see what had happened.

Slowly, Molly opened her eyes a little bit. Then she closed them again. She could only bear to let the bright, sunny world in bit by bit. For although everyone else's world was exactly as it had always been, hers was in turmoil, and she wasn't sure how she could manage it. Finally she spoke, because she felt it might be best for someone to say something.

"Oh, Maudie, tell me this is a terrible dream."

But Maude could not tell her that. She could only beat her tail anxiously on the ground.

"Well, at least I'm not alone. At least there's you, Maude. And Claudine, I guess." And she sighed—Claudine was a very poor replacement for what she had lost.

Lost? Had she lost her mama? Was that what had happened? Molly sat up and rubbed at her eyes. She pinched her arm. Yes, she was definitely awake. She gazed up at the tree.

It was a beautiful tree, tall and spreading and not quite one type or another. Its leaves, in fact, were not the same type at all. Some resembled an oak's leaves, others had a reddish tone, and some were dark green and small. As she stared up into the canopy, it seemed that all the leaves shook at once and the sun fell through them like diamonds.

"Mama?" she whispered. "Is that you?"

The straw hat twirled on the end of its branch.

Molly felt something. At least she thought she did. What was it, though? Could it be a vibration? She moved closer to the tree and rested her cheek against its trunk.

"Mama, is that you in there?"

There was almost a murmur within the trunk, Molly was certain.

"Maudie," she declared, "this tree is Mama, and she is alive. All we have to do is work out how to change her back!"

Maude pricked her ears and sat at Molly's feet, awaiting instruction, while Claudine walked stealthily around the trunk of the tree, uttering a few startled meows.

"Yes, that's all," repeated Molly to herself. She had forgotten how to make potions. She had purposefully taken no interest in such matters, and until now she had never wanted to feel vibrations.

Molly let go of the tree and marched inside with pretend confidence. She went straight to her mama's desk. Perhaps her mama had left instructions for how to reverse the magic.

Drifts of books and notes and diagrams covered the desk in uneven piles. Molly began searching through them. The red notebook was the one her mama had been using last. In it were pictures of plants, information about their uses—all the usual stuff. But nothing about the acorn potion.

Molly stood up. She felt unsteady. If there was no recipe for turning her mama back into a mama, how would she get her back? And until she did, what would she do without her?

She flung open the cupboard to see what food was there, for one thing. The bread bin was empty. There was no yogurt in the fridge; they had eaten it all last night with the stewed apricots. Molly thought longingly of the black-eyed pea autumn stew her mama always made. How did she make it? Molly should have paid more attention. She took down a jar of cashews and shook some into her hand. Her mama made cashew paste and mixed it with chocolate and coconut and rolled it into balls. Molly knew how to make those. She would make hundreds of them. And there was still the last crumpet.

Molly went out to the vegetable garden. She stared at a large zucchini and pinched it. She didn't want the zucchini to know it, but the truth was, she didn't like zucchini much, or pumpkin. Mulberries, she thought happily, and ran to the mulberry tree to check there were still plenty there. The birds loved them too. Molly dragged the ladder to the tree and climbed up with the orange bucket to gather as many as possible.

"Sorry, birds," she called out. "These are desperate times." From high up in the mulberry tree, she glanced cautiously toward the Mama tree, which stood rather proudly above all the others, except the pines.

The Mama tree was not solemn and dark like the pines; it shimmered and shook as if the leaves were conversing loudly, laughing perhaps, even uproariously. Molly sighed. At least the Mama tree seemed happy and well, and with the sun hat crowning it, it looked beautiful, and special, and different from any other tree.

Molly climbed down; her dress was smirched with purple juice. She went inside and plonked the bucket of mulberries on the bench. Now she would make the chocolate-and-cashew balls, and they would be sweeter and bigger than ever before.

"After all, Maude," she said, "we need some cheering up right now."

Lavender

CHAPTER 9

THE DARK

Molly spent the afternoon making chocolate-and-cashew balls and writing an urgent letter to her brother Miro, as she didn't have an address for Yip.

"Dear Miro," she wrote,

> *Please can you help? Mama has accidentally turned herself into a tree and I don't know how to turn her back. She is still there because I can hear her humming through the tree. You should see the tree she has become. Very tall and spreading but muddled about what its leaves should be of course. I know you are not good at*

this sort of magic, but if you came and played
your trumpet, it might help. She would hear it.
Also, remember when you made birdhouses for
birds to nest in? And you climbed up in trees all
around and installed them? Well, maybe this
is something too. Maybe the birds are grateful.
Maybe they can help. If you see Yip, please tell
him what has happened. Anyway, it's been a
while since either of you came home. Do you have
some new dishes to cook, because I am hungry?

Love from Molly (Little Pump)

She put "Little Pump" in parentheses, as she was big enough now not to be referred to as the Little Pump, but it was what her brothers called her still, since they hadn't seen how much she had grown.

She walked down to the letter box and posted the letter and then came home and emptied the fridge of all the things she wouldn't eat: broccoli, cabbage, goat cheese, pickled lemons, umeboshi paste, and fennel. That could all go to the chickens. For herself and Maude, she heaped chocolate balls and mulberries onto plates and put them in the fridge. Molly suddenly felt important and grown-up and responsible. She patted Maude reassuringly and said, "Now, now,

47

Maudie, everything will be okay." Even though she wasn't certain about this, it made her feel better to say it. But the better she felt, the more she began to think that when her mama did come back, she wouldn't be happy to see the fridge so full of chocolate balls, so Molly stuck the broccoli back in, just in case.

Then she made a little feast of chocolate balls and biscuits with squished mulberries and honey for herself, Maude, and Claudine. She set the table outside with the special-occasion lilac tablecloth, and she picked some lavender and jammed it into the yellow milk jug and put it in the middle. It was just as Mama would have done it, she thought, and she called out, just as her mama might have, "Everyone, lunch is ready."

Maude and Claudine didn't come running, as proper children should, but then again, thought Molly, often real children didn't come straightaway anyway, especially if they were in the middle of a small adventure. So she called them again, and in the end she went and fetched Claudine, who jumped up on the table and sniffed disapprovingly at the mulberry and honey biscuits, and then, with a flick of her tail, jumped down and returned to basking in the sun. Maude sat by Molly's side and ate biscuits under the table from Molly's hand. Molly stared out down the hill, where the Mama tree seemed now to have grown even larger. She wasn't hungry after all, and perhaps she even felt a little lonely. From where she sat the tree seemed to take all the attention. A whole new reaching and spreading shape in the sky. The Mama tree certainly did block out the neighbors. And it was lovely.

But it was odd to have a meal without anyone who spoke or sat at the table. Perhaps she would invite Ellen for lunch. But she couldn't without explaining that her mama had become a tree. And Ellen would have trouble believing her. Or, if Ellen did believe her, what would she think? Would she go home and tell her mother that Molly was imagining things? Molly frowned to herself as she pictured this.

The fact was, if anyone came over, they would soon realize there was no Mama, and Molly would have to explain what had happened, and then she'd be taken away to an orphanage.

"Oh, Mama," she said out loud, with a great sigh and a good dash of fondness too. And then she went and curled up on her mama's bed. She sank into a soft cloud of familiar Mama scents. Soon she would get up and do something, but first she would lie awhile and think about what to do.

Maude jumped up on the bed, but Claudine stayed

on top of the piano and sulked, as she was hungry and she didn't like chocolate balls.

When Molly woke up, her arms were cold. The house was shadowy and lit with the last blob of light. Molly sat up as the memory of what had happened to her mama burst into her mind, and she flung her hands over her eyes and willed it all away. The evening sounds crept around her and she shivered. She rummaged in her mama's drawers for a cardigan. Outside, the sky was sinking toward darkness and windows were glowing with insideness. Dinners were being cooked, probably nice tomato and lentil stews, the sort Molly would be having for dinner if her mama hadn't turned into a tree, and possibly even apple crumbles. Molly's tummy rumbled. Being alone during the day was one thing, but darkness was frightening. Anything could come out of the darkness.

Claudine meowed loudly. Molly stomped to the

fridge, where she found some milk. "Well, Claudine, that's the last of the milk, so you better get used to biscuits and mulberries like the rest of us."

Claudine ignored this comment and lapped her milk contentedly.

Molly and Maude went outside and ate some more of the chocolate-ball feast, which was still waiting there for someone. Molly tried very much to enjoy it, especially since she could eat as many of the treats as she liked. But having so many wasn't actually as wonderful as she had imagined. After five, she was already sick of chocolate-and-cashew balls. It was probably the fault of the dark, which now fell over everything. The trees began to whisper, the grass had turned black, and the sky shuddered as the chill crept into the air. Molly pushed the plate of chocolate balls away. She called Maude and snuggled close.

"Maudie," she said, "don't be frightened; it's only the night. There's nothing to be afraid of."

But Maude wasn't frightened. Maude was alert. Her ears stood up and she quivered as if she was listening to something. Molly's heart quivered too. Was there someone there in the paddock beneath them? She buried her face in Maude's ears. She didn't want to look, but the longer she sat, still not looking, the more frightened she became. She lifted her head. The garden was still; the trees looked like dark figures.

"I know you, trees," Molly called out. Her voice shook, and the darkness seemed to swallow it easily. She tried again. "Don't pretend. Don't pretend to be anything you're not, because I know."

Nothing moved. Not a breath of wind shook a leaf in response. Perhaps it was the stillness that made things eerie and unnatural.

Move, thought Molly. Move! She stepped off the veranda and began to windmill her arms, just to stir up the air. "Whatever is about to happen, happen now," she declared with an authority that surprised her. She had even stomped her foot so that the earth could hear it too. Her arms stretched out, her fingers wiggled, combing the air for clues.

Maude whined. And then, as if Molly had indeed been heard, there came a great rustling and, in the same instant, the Mama tree lit up in a silvery glow. It was as if a solitary moonbeam had swung its ray directly onto the Mama tree. The leaves glittered and sprang into action, fluttering and whispering, so that the tree seemed to be cheerfully waving its arms about and saying, "Look, here I am."

Without knowing why, and as if entranced, Molly walked toward it. Maude followed her, flat-backed and stalking, ears pricked. Somehow the closer she went to the tree, the safer Molly felt. The ground hummed; leaves whirled in the windless night. The Mama tree was as pale and luminous as the moon itself. Molly pressed her ear to the trunk. It was warm.

"Mama?" she whispered. "Mama, are you there?"

The humming she felt in the ground now swelled in the trunk and became stronger, as if it had rushed to answer her question.

Molly pressed closer. She listened harder. The humming was more a feeling, a trembling, pounding sort of vibration. And it came in waves; it rose and fell away, as if it was a signal. Was it her mama's voice?

Molly turned to Maude. "Maude, tonight we'll sleep here. I think Mama needs us."

She hardly waited for Maude to agree before she hurried back to the house to gather the bedding. She took the pillow and cushions and covers off her bed and dragged them to the tree. She ran back for Maude's basket. Then she went back, for a third time, and put in the washing basket the ukulele, her collection of

small rocks, her string of silver
flowers, and her mama's alarm
clock. She looked at Claudine, who was watching
with her usual bored and
superior air.

"Well, Claudine, you'll have to make up your own
mind, but Maudie and I are sleeping with Mama. And
if you don't come too, it will be just you all alone, just
you and the dark night."

Molly tried to make it sound awful to be left in
the house, but Claudine didn't even raise her nose in
response.

"You pretend nothing worries you, but I know it
does," said Molly, and she flounced out the door and
slammed it slightly to make a proper show of her de-
parture.

The air buzzed and creaked with the activities of
insects, and the Mama tree rustled and shone. Molly
hung up her string of silver flowers and stashed her
rock collection in the crook of a branch, and then she
made her bed on the ground beneath and jumped in.

She lay there on her back. The tree's branches
were like a roof above her. Could her mama see her?
Did trees see? Molly closed her eyes and imagined
she was a tree too; she urged her feelings toward the

Mama tree. A loud creaking sounded above her, and the leaves rustled with a new vigor.

Maude jumped up with a bark. Molly sat up too. Something had happened. Maude's tail sagged and lifted, as if uncertain what response it should make.

The tree was changing. Three large branches were lining themselves up evenly right above Molly, like a roof. Or even a platform. Molly knew instantly what it was. It was her mama reaching toward her.

Molly smiled. She threw her pillow and quilt up over the branches and then scrambled up the trunk and lay down across them.

It was very uncomfortable, and no doubt anyone else would have preferred to sleep on a mattress, but Molly felt so very safe all of a sudden that she hardly noticed. In fact, it seemed to her that she was lying again in her mama's arms. She closed her eyes and whispered, "Good night, Mama tree."

Sow Thistle

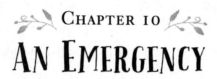

CHAPTER 10
AN EMERGENCY

The next morning Molly crossed the dry creek bed at the bottom of her street and climbed up the other side, and she followed the road all the way to Ellen's place. Ellen Palmer's house stood on a flat block of shaved lawn, with a couple of stone pathways lined with clumps of Easter daisy. The trampoline in the front was caged in blue net and stood rather forlornly beside a glorious loquat tree. Underneath it were two timid gray rabbits (Batman and Barbie) in a hutch with a chicken-wire roof, which Maude stood over, transfixed.

All Molly knew was that she needed to talk to someone, and since Ellen was her best friend, Ellen was the person she steered herself toward. But now that Molly had arrived, she wasn't sure if she really wanted to go inside. There was the house that she had always admired, square and solid and with a certain look of neatness and completion, and there was she, adrift in a mystical turn of events and swirling with fears. She was messy and giddy, and hungry too. Twigs were tangled in her hair. And Ellen's house seemed like it wouldn't have room for such whirling and tangling. It had never felt like that before, but now everything was so different and unstuck in Molly's life.

Molly crept around the side of the house to Ellen's bedroom window. Perhaps she could just whisper to Ellen to come out. Perhaps she need not go inside. Ellen's curtain was drawn, so Molly tapped quietly at the window, but Maude barked, as if frustrated with all this cautious behavior.

The curtain was pulled back and there stood Ellen Palmer with a glittery yellow hair band and blue eye shadow. She gaped at Molly and opened the window.

"Molly, what are you doing? I'm dressing up."

"I didn't want to come in the front door."

"Did your mum bring you?"

"No, I just came with Maude."

Ellen lifted up her foot and showed it to Molly. She wore a sequined shoe. "But did your mum let you come here by yourself?"

"Well, yes." Molly ignored the sequined shoe. She moved closer to the window and held on to the ledge. "Mama couldn't talk, though."

Ellen said nothing while she puzzled over this. She moved her mouth from side to side.

"Is she sick? Did you walk all the way?"

"Yes, she's sick," said Molly. She wasn't sure now why she had come and what she should say. She had thought maybe Ellen would know what to do. But as she stood outside Ellen's window, she felt that if she said, "My mama is a tree," her friend might not believe that such a thing could even happen. Molly looked at her. Could she believe?

Ellen shrugged. "Lucky you. That means you can do anything you want." Ellen shook her hair, which was frizzy from her plaits. "Are you coming in? We could make up a song." She started to sing.

Molly sighed. She wasn't in the mood for making up songs.

"Are you okay, Molly?" said Ellen flatly. She folded

her arms over on the window ledge and moved closer. She was concerned. She could sense that Molly was not her usual self.

Molly panicked. She couldn't tell Ellen her mama had turned into a tree. At the very least Ellen would be horrified. Molly felt she couldn't let it get to that. She was not ready for it to be horrifying, because in the middle of all that horror, there was a quiet, tremulous hum, and that was Molly's own mama.

"I'm fine, and Mama is not technically sick, she's gone away. An emergency," declared Molly with sudden assurance.

"An emergency?" Ellen frowned. This was all too confusing.

Molly leaned in the window and whispered, "Yes, an emergency. It's kind of secret, though. It's to do with my brothers. She had to go to Cuba, in fact. So I'm at home looking after Maude."

"All by yourself?" Ellen gasped. Her hand flew to her mouth. She seemed immensely pleased and excited. "Well, why don't I come and stay with you, to keep you company?"

"No." Molly shook her head instantly, and Ellen flinched. She looked taken aback. Molly was flustered. The conversation had taken her down into a hole she didn't know how to get out of. "It's just that . . . well . . . I think this is something I have to do on my own. And you mustn't tell your mum. Promise? It's a real secret."

Ellen stared at Molly, as if searching for a reason.

Molly knew that her story had all come out in a shoddy, made-up way and that Ellen had sensed the falseness in it. Molly hadn't found the relief she was looking for. So now there was a flat, awkward feeling between them, and it was all Molly's fault because she ought to have told Ellen the truth or said nothing at all. She edged away from the window.

Ellen leaned out. "Wait!" She disappeared from the window and then came back with two mandarins and an apricot muesli bar. "Here, for your lunch tomorrow." She offered a small grin. Molly knew Ellen wanted to help. The offering of food was her gentle, birdlike way of saying, "I am here."

Molly walked quickly home. There was a time when an apricot muesli bar would have made her very happy, but now she stared at it crossly. It meant nothing after all. It wouldn't change anything. Her mama was a tree and Molly was alone, and an apricot muesli bar was after all nothing but some oats glued together with sugar.

What she needed was a potion, a thing of real magic, a deep and important mysterious thing that was connected to the ways of the natural world.

That was the only way to turn her mama back.

Magpie

CHAPTER 11

THE TRUTH

Molly missed the next few days of school. She couldn't imagine how she could concentrate on math or anything when her mind was in such a commotion. She needed to focus all her attention on getting her mama back.

The branches of the Mama tree had sprouted a mass of soft leaves that wove themselves together like a nest and not only cushioned Molly but also wrapped around her as she slept. Yet, try as she might, Molly couldn't get Maude up into the tree, and this left Maude pacing at its base. Molly was also getting sick of chocolate-and-cashew balls, and she had finished all the mulberries. She and Maude ate the last of the honey on biscuits and some tomatoes from the garden, and Claudine ate the blackberry jam, as it was all she would tolerate. Molly watched her lick the jar.

"You're very spoiled, Claudine. Watch out, because all that jam will make you a fat cat."

Claudine was already nicely plump and showed no signs of worrying about being fat. Probably, thought Molly, it suited her a little anyway.

Molly sat cross-legged in her nest in the tree. A raucous gang of cockatoos swooped into the leaves and landed high in the boughs. Sun splattered and glistened through the leaves. And the straw hat twirled on its branch.

Suddenly, Prudence Grimshaw shot out from her house. She cast an angry glance at the tree, as if something had alerted her to Molly's presence there. But, although she stared hungrily and then searched the tree with her darting eyes, she couldn't see Molly.

Molly sat perfectly still and hardly dared breathe. Eventually, Prudence Grimshaw frowned, gave a snort, and disappeared into the shed.

Molly closed her eyes and rested her hands on

the branch. She listened. Cars purred in the distance, birds sang and screeched, air hummed in the leaves, branches creaked, and from the base of the tree came a reluctant *humph* as Maude plonked herself down. Molly listened and listened, but she couldn't hear her mama. Instead, the sounds faded and thoughts drifted through her head.

The thoughts were disconnected. They came in waves, and Molly felt tired as she tried to work them out. The Grimshaws, Claudine licking the jam, lying to Ellen, Pim Wilder and the paper angel, the ball of mud—were they all connected? Why had her world fallen into small pieces like a jigsaw puzzle scattered over the floor?

She pressed her mind back to the tree. Branches wobbled, and bright patches of sky swayed above. The wet, dirt smell of bark and leaves mingled with the air. All tree business as usual.

Why couldn't she hear her mama? Perhaps she was trying too hard. Things never came when she tried too hard to get them. What she needed was a walk. That was what her mama always did when she had some thoughts that she needed to set free. Not only that—Maude needed a walk too. Molly jumped down from the tree.

"Come on, Maudie. Let's go to the creek."

They crossed the rickety bridge and Maude ran at a heron that was perched on the railing. The bird swerved off down the throat of the creek, which was full of reeds. The water slipped over the rocks and pooled at the tufts of bulrush. There was a steep bank on each side that rose up to become a stout brick wall.

Molly took off her sandals and walked along the wall. It was such a fat, smooth, sun-warmed wall that she lay down on it on her tummy, dangling one arm over the side, letting the warmth of the bricks soak into her cheek.

Out of the daze of blue sky and croaking frogs came a voice.

"Are you waiting for the sky to fall?"

Molly propped herself up on her elbows.

Pim Wilder was framed by the blue sky, his face dark with shadows. He sat on his bike with one foot on the wall. He wasn't wearing the school top, but a T-shirt with stripes, which gave him the air of a drunken sailor.

He looked at Molly as if he expected her to be either frightened or annoyed by his question, and would almost enjoy it if she was.

Molly, who had now successfully faced the night

alone, reminded herself that Pim Wilder was only a
boy and not nearly as frightening as the dark. She
scrambled to her knees.

"I saw you at the park. You had a ball of dirt in your
hand," she said. It was best when feeling nervous or
timid to behave in the exact opposite way.

Pim was not deterred at all. He laughed. "Not dirt.
It was a pellet. There's a powerful owl nesting in that
tree. That's how you tell."

Only Pim Wilder could turn a ball of dirt into a
whole journey of discovery. Molly resented and admired him for it, both at the same time.

"They swallow their prey whole or in large chunks
and then they spew up these little pellets of fur and
bones, and if you look closely, you can work out what
they ate. I reckon that one had eaten a sugar glider or
a ringtail. The bones were bigger than a bird's. They
eat kookaburras too, and parrots."

Molly didn't like to think of sugar
gliders or parrots being swallowed in
chunks. She made a face to show this
was disgusting, but Pim hardly noticed.

"Have you heard a powerful owl
call? It's like this." He cupped his
hands to his mouth and uttered two

mournful hoots. "It's the only one that sounds sad, like a real owl call."

"And is it sad?"

"Who knows? I doubt it, though. There's nothing to be sad about if you are an owl."

"How can you know?" Molly almost wouldn't have been surprised if Pim claimed he once was an owl. But he didn't. Instead, he seemed amused by her question. He leaned his bike against the wall and sat down.

Molly plucked a stalk of grass from the crack in the bricks and twisted it. She had said something that interested him.

"What about a baby owl who lost its mother? It would be sad," she continued.

Pim stared at her. "Probably frightened more than anything, but I guess it would have to learn a thing or two pretty quickly. Did you skip school today?"

"My mum's gone away," Molly said.

"What about your dad?"

"He went away a long time ago." Molly tried to sound breezy. How strange that she was even telling him.

Pim leaned forward. His expression glittered with curiosity. "So who is looking after you?"

Molly tossed her piece of grass into the creek. "I'm looking after myself," she sang.

Pim straightened up. He looked at her closely, as if to check she was the person he thought she was. His eyes were clear and piercing, but they were grinning at her too.

Molly stood up and jumped off the wall, as if to shake off his gaze. Maude stood next to her. "And I've been eating as many chocolate balls as I like, for breakfast, lunch, and dinner," she added.

Pim let out a laugh.

"Your mum goes away and leaves you all by yourself, and you stop going to school and eat chocolate balls for breakfast. That's kind of weird."

Pim Wilder could see right inside her. Molly's face was hot.

"I'm not weird," she said, mustering more certainty than she really felt. And then, despite her doubts, or because of them, she spun around elegantly on her heel and began to walk away.

"Well, that's a pity," he called out. "I was just beginning to think at least one person around here might be interesting."

Molly stopped. She turned back and shouted, "I am interesting. And I'm in a really interesting situation. So interesting you probably wouldn't be able to believe it if I told you."

He walked his bike up to her. "Try me," he said.

And because he said it softly, and because he looked at her without any thought written on his face, but with the sort of blankness of an open window, Molly stopped.

Could she tell him? Could she tell Pim Wilder? Was this the right thing to do? She hadn't even told Ellen, and Ellen was her best friend. But perhaps Pim Wilder was the only person who might be able to know such a thing and not be afraid of it.

"First, promise you won't tell anyone else. And promise to believe me too."

He opened his palms and lifted them toward her as if he was ready to take the weight of anything she might say.

"I promise."

Molly took a deep breath. She put her hand on Maude's head. She frowned.

"My mama accidentally turned herself into a tree."

She'd said it. The truth had been plonked right there on the shining gravel pathway between them. Molly shut her eyes against it and stood unsteadily, the sun flaring across her eyelids and making everything feel hot and scorched and indistinct. She felt she might cry, and because she didn't want to, she rubbed at her eyes and blinked them open again.

There was Pim Wilder, dark and still, surrounded

by the bright, hazy light. He moved one step toward her, as if he thought she might fall. Molly hugged her arms around herself and her lip trembled.

Pim stared back at her. His mouth had dropped open, and his eyes were round and green and full of wonder.

She knew he believed her.

Chamomile

CHAPTER 12
GREEN-BEAN FRUIT

Molly and Pim stood at the base of the tree. Pim craned his neck and looked up through the leaves.

"Wow," he breathed. "The leaves are all different types. It's . . . well, it's an amazing tree. I mean she, your mother, the tree, I don't know, it's something. You can tell that." He shook his head, perplexed. He touched the trunk, then walked around it, as if somewhere there might be a clue that Molly hadn't uncovered.

Molly watched him. If it was this amazing to Pim Wilder, how would it be to everyone else? The Mama tree was startling and different from other trees, and sooner or later it would be noticed.

Of course, she thought with a sigh. Of course her mama couldn't have become an unremarkable tree, an ordinary tree. Because her mama wasn't an ordinary person. Molly leaped toward the trunk and, pressing her back to it, she held her palms against it protectively.

"You can't tell anyone," Molly said. "Imagine what they might do if—"

"Of course I won't." Pim stepped back. He shoved his hands into his pockets. "But, Molly," he whispered, "what are you going to do? I mean, what about your dad, for one thing? Can't he help? Is he into this stuff too?"

Molly shook her head firmly. "Oh, my dad, my dad . . ."

She felt confused. Her foot dug at the ground. She half wanted to tell him all about her dad, and she half wanted not to speak of him at all. "He's lost somewhere in Cuba. He doesn't know about potions anyway. My brothers know a bit, but they're far away too." She shrugged, as if it meant nothing.

Pim put his finger to the back of his ear, puzzled. "So, your mother is a tree. And no one knows. No one except me."

Molly could tell that he was struggling to make sense of it. She hoped he wasn't going to try to comfort her.

"I only told you because I wanted to ask you if you had some spare dog food for Maudie and Claudine. Well, Claudine is a cat, but she will have to put up with dog food, as it's going to be hard times for a while around here. But don't worry about me. Look where I sleep."

Molly then expertly hoisted herself up into her nest of branches and leaves and peeped back over at him. "Only problem is Maudie can't get here."

"You sleep there?"

Pim stood still, struck again, and Molly thought he looked at her with admiration. She ducked down in her nest of leaves.

Pim began to pace again. "Of course I'll get some dog food. But you can't sleep there forever. I mean, it must be pretty great sleeping in a tree, but winter will be brutal. And anyway, we have to find a way to turn your mother back. Don't we?"

He'd said "*we* have to find a way." Did that mean he

was going to help her? Could he help? Molly perked up. She peered over her nest. Pim was frowning, as if already entrenched in thoughts about how to get her mama back.

Molly felt suddenly very tired and very relieved, and she let go of something inside herself, something that she had been holding on to firmly. Her whole body felt limp, but it roared with sudden hunger too. Below her, Pim seemed to be gauging the size of things with his arms.

Of all the people, she thought, of all the people to share her biggest-ever problem. But there he was, with his loose striped T-shirt, tapping at the trunk of the tree, already getting to work in some way. The thing about Pim was that he seemed to like working things out and he was eager. But, best of all, he wasn't going to tell anyone. Molly climbed down from her perch.

"I'm really hungry," she said. Her head felt strange and light. She hadn't meant to say it out loud: she had just thought it and said it all at once, suddenly realizing why she felt funny and not right and as if anything, any little thing, might blow her over.

Pim stood up and scratched his head. "I'm going back to my house. I'll get some rope and some food and bring them back before it gets dark."

Before Molly could ask him about the rope, the

tree began to make a noise, as if a wind had swept through it. But there was no wind. The branches trembled on their own, and neither Molly nor Pim knew whether it was the late-afternoon light glowing through the leaves or whether the colors just suddenly became more vivid. As they watched, small pale-pink buds burst at the tips of the branches. They began to swell and grow plump and roundish, until they hung pendulously like blood-plum-colored mangoes. The tree slowly became still again, and the strange fruit hung there, wobbling slightly.

"Wow," said Pim. His hands shot to the top of his head, and he half crouched, as if sheltering from the strangeness. He turned to Molly, his eyes burning with excitement. "I guess you're used to this sort of stuff."

Molly shook her head slowly. "No, not really. Not at all. But I wonder . . ."

"What?" Pim took his hands from his head and straightened up. He gazed at the tree, which now looked even more magnificent.

Molly reached up to the lowest-hanging fruit. The skin was firm. She pressed her nose to it, and because it smelled good, she pulled it off.

"I wonder if Mama heard me say that I was hungry."

"You think she grew these for you to eat?" Pim reached up and touched one, but he didn't pick it.

"If I lie in the tree, I can feel her there, so I'm sure she can sense me too. I think I can communicate with her, in a way." Molly blushed. It embarrassed her to admit this. Boys didn't really talk to their mums at all, let alone communicate through bark, but perhaps in this way, as in most ways, Pim was different. Perhaps Pim Wilder was the one person who wouldn't think it so weird to talk to a tree.

But Pim whistled and gazed in wonder at Molly and then at the tree, as if all this was exactly the sort of thing he found interesting, and then he rocked back and forth on his heels and blew out a long breath.

"You should definitely eat it, then," he said.

Molly dug her fingers into the skin. It was hard, almost like the bark of a tree, but underneath it was a moist green inner casing. She tasted a bit of it.

Green beans, she thought, it's just like green beans.

Beneath the green bit was soft, creamy flesh, which came easily away from a shiny brown pit. It was sweet and juicy, with a hint of nuttiness.

"What's it like?"

Molly handed it to Pim. "Try it. The white bit is delicious. It's like lychees and almonds and vanilla custard. The green bit is like—"

"Green beans! Exactly like green beans," Pim

laughed. "Next thing we know, we'll turn into a tree too, or a frog or something."

Molly almost laughed, but her mouth was full. She ate the whole fruit, even the green-bean part. And then she ate another. She had no fear of turning into a frog.

"Of course. Mama made it like green beans because she always wants me to eat green vegetables."

Molly felt better. Was it the fruit or the feeling that her mama was still there, still looking after her? She felt hopeful and warm, and she opened a little more to the mysterious, whispering forces that had swallowed her mama.

Pim stared at her. Could he see? Could he sense them too? His gaze fixed on Molly, his eyes flashing with thoughts. It was the look that frightened others, but Molly didn't feel afraid. She had nothing more to hide now. She took a bite of her fruit and stared straight back at him.

Pim grinned. "You eat it," he said. "I've already got a mother forcing green beans into me. I'm going to get that dog food." He turned to go.

Molly watched him walk away. His odd, loping walk, as if his legs were made of string, was familiar in a way, but now he seemed different. Maybe it was just that she saw him differently because he had become the only person who knew. Somehow Molly knew he was exactly the right person to know. She reached up to pick more fruit and sat at the base of the tree, leaning her back against it.

"Thank you, Mama," she whispered. "But I'd like it if you came back now and made some black-eyed pea stew."

Apple Tree

CHAPTER 13
A LETTER

Finally there was a proper team: Molly, Pim, Maude, and, somewhere prowling the outskirts, Claudine. Claudine had watched the bursting of the fruit from the veranda. She lay on the daybed, stretching every now and then as if she was more interested in the look of her paws than the activities in the tree. But, still, Molly didn't have high expectations of Claudine. What did feel odd was that Ellen wasn't part of the team. Ellen was always Molly's first choice for anything.

Molly took Maude to the wild orchard that spread over the creek flats. She took Mama's basket with her and she picked some peaches. Then she climbed down the other side of the hill to the oval, and she watched some schoolkids playing cricket. When she tired of this, she and Maude wandered up the path by the railway, and Molly swished at the clumps of long grasses with a stick and scavenged some last blackberries.

On the way home she climbed the back fence of Mrs. Mulligan's overgrown garden, while Maude ran around the long way, and she picked some blood plums. Mrs. Mulligan was too old to pick them herself. Molly left a pile of them on the back doorstep with some peaches too. She didn't feel like talking to Mrs. Mulligan, though. She liked feeling she was captain of her own evening, and she walked slowly back along the street, as the windows of houses began to light up.

Once back at her own house, Molly cut up the remaining peaches and plums and put them in a pot with some honey and cinnamon to stew. Then she decided to serenade Maude with her ukulele while she waited for the fruit to cook. It was always nice to sing to Maude, as Maude wasn't superior like Claudine, and she didn't try to sing along like

Mama did. Molly sang long and loudly and almost let the peaches burn.

"Don't worry, I'll get better at cooking," Molly said to Maude after they'd eaten the stewed fruit. Then they scrambled through the garden to the Mama tree, which waited quietly for them even though something had changed while they were out.

There was now an elaborate pulley system slung over the lowest tree branch, and attached to it was a small wooden platform on which Maude's basket had been wedged. In the basket were two fruit buns, a can of dog food, a picture of a powerful owl, and a flashlight.

Molly grinned. Pim had obviously been there. She plonked herself down and ate a whole bun immediately. She gave the other one to Maude and patted the basket for her to get in. And then Molly stood on the ground and pulled on the rope. The basket rose. Maude jumped out immediately, and it took Molly quite a few goes to coax her into staying in till it got all the way up to the nest. Molly climbed up and made a hole in the owl picture so she could hang it from a twig.

Now the dark had begun to fall. Birds made their last noisy swoops through the garden. The sky had turned lilac and dusty and then the clinging black.

Molly turned on the flashlight and aimed the beam in arcs up through the leaves. Maude curled up beside her. Molly hadn't brushed her teeth or had a shower, and she thought how nice it was not to have to do anything at all. In fact, she could stay awake all night long if she wanted to. She stared up at the stars peeping through the leaves. She could watch them through the night, see what they did. But stargazing made her tired, and she fell asleep almost immediately.

Maude woke Molly early the next morning by barking.

"What now, Maude? Are you just happy to be up in the Mama tree or is there someone here?"

The day was crisp again and seemed all polished and winking clean with sunshine. Molly lowered Maude in the basket and then swung herself down. She had developed quite a stylish and acrobatic sort of way of getting up and down from her platform. If someone was here, it was probably Pim Wilder.

But it wasn't Pim. It was Prudence Grimshaw. She was rapping urgently on the door to the house and leaning to peer in the window all at once. Molly recognized the short, colorless hair and the gray clothes that made her look ghostly and drab, as if she had arrived out of a dismal future.

"There's no one home," said Molly loudly.

Prudence Grimshaw gave a start and turned sharply, clutching an envelope at her neck. She looked embarrassed at being caught peering inside, but then she gathered herself and pursed her thin lips indignantly, as if Molly should not have crept up behind her and given her such a fright.

"Where is your mother?" she demanded.

"Mama is out," replied Molly.

Maude let out a short bark as if to second this, and Prudence Grimshaw jumped again.

"Well, when will she be back? I have to give her this letter."

"You can give it to me and I'll give it to her." Molly reached out her hand.

Prudence Grimshaw held on fast to the letter and dipped her head very slowly as if to show her control over the situation.

"It is a very important letter," she warned. "It's about that . . . that . . . that tree." She ejected the word "tree" with a shriek, and her arm swung up and stiffened accusingly as she pointed and glared ferociously at the Mama tree. The Mama tree did not shirk or blush.

Molly said nothing, but she began to feel very worried. Prudence Grimshaw dropped her arm and nodded her head with a there-you-have-it motion, and then she straightened her gray skirt and began to speak again.

"Half of it is actually on our property. I can't allow it. I won't allow it. The mess!" She added this last bit about the mess with a pointedly pompous tone, which made Molly imagine her sipping tea and using a red pen to cross out words on someone else's writing.

Molly glared back at her and felt almost ready to charge. But she said nothing and only puffed out her nostrils to show her irritation. Prudence Grimshaw's brow arched, and she thrust the letter at Molly.

"The letter demands that your mother has the overhanging branches cut off. Make sure she gets it."

Molly shook her head and stood up tall. "But we can't cut off the branches. How would you like it if we cut off *your* arms?"

The woman snorted. "A tree does not have arms!" She handed the letter to Molly and turned to go. But she looked back with a sly frown. "Shouldn't you be getting ready for school? There's obviously a lot you haven't yet learned. A tree with arms—I never heard such a ridiculous notion."

"And there's a lot you haven't learned too, like how to be nice, for one thing," burst out Molly.

Prudence Grimshaw's chin began to quiver. Her eyebrows did a jagged dance, and her breath came out in short, rising snorts. "Well," she said, and huffed loudly, "you . . . you should learn some respect."

So should you, thought Molly, but she held her mouth firmly shut and kicked at some dry leaves that lay on the path. Then she swiveled around and tore back down the path to the Mama tree.

Once she was back in the tree, Molly tore open the envelope and read the letter.

> *Dear Madam,*
> *The obnoxious tree that has suddenly grown on the border of our property has many branches overhanging our property. We demand that you remove these branches immediately. If this is not done by Saturday, we will be forced to cut them off ourselves, at your expense, and if they continue to grow, we will take action to remove the whole tree.*
> *P. & E. Grimshaw*

Wishing Tree

CHAPTER 14
THE BATTLE CRY

M olly folded her arms across her chest. I'll tear the limbs off anyone who comes near us with a chain saw, she thought. And then she pictured herself chained to the branches, staring down at crabby old Prudence Grimshaw with her thin nose and pointy eyebrows and her sharp elbows and shrill indignation.

Nothing—thought Molly bravely as she dodged an imaginary knife flung from Prudence Grimshaw's cold heart—nothing, nothing, nothing will move me from this tree.

"From you, Mama," she said out loud, correcting herself. "Nothing will remove me from you."

Molly lay down as if to shelter the Mama tree with her body, and she clung to the tree because she felt very upset. Her world seemed to have been eaten up by Grimshaws, chain saws, and loneliness. She tried to close her mind's eye. She wrapped both arms tightly around the branch that held her and squeezed everything she had toward it.

And that was how Pim Wilder found her.

"Hiya," he called softly, as if not wanting to startle her. "You coming to school?"

Molly lifted her head, but she didn't uncurl herself from the branch.

"Something terrible has happened," she declared with a sniff.

Pim took a step closer. "What's happened?" Pim's voice was steady and reassuring and even familiar now.

Molly uncurled herself and sat on her platform, looking down at him. "The Grimshaws are going to cut off the branches. Mama's branches! They could be Mama's arms." She clutched again at the nearby branch with one hand and with the other she waved the letter. Then she folded her arms and lifted her chin. "I'm going to chain myself here and never come down."

Pim blew out a low, whistling breath. "You're gonna get pretty tired of holding on."

Molly glared at him.

Pim frowned back. He scratched his head and blinked into the sun, which had risen behind the Mama tree and given it a momentous quality. Its long, dark branches swept up toward the sky and its leaves glistened. Molly sat clinging on like a limpet, full of resistance.

In that moment, Pim looked at her as if he understood something that she didn't. This just made Molly crosser. He couldn't be counted on to react properly. He was not looking like someone who had just been told of imminent disaster, or like someone who realized that he stood on the brink of a great battle. Pim Wilder just looked calmly interested.

Molly frowned and looked away. She shouldn't have relied on Pim Wilder. Her problem was catastrophic. She plucked a fruit off the branch. Now that Pim had returned, so had her appetite. The weirdest boy at school was now making things look normal and possible. It was confusing. Confusing and catastrophic and strange. She bit hungrily into the green-bean fruit.

Pim's voice sailed up into the tree. "You know, you look like a little stray cat stuck up there."

"I don't care how I look. I've got more important things to worry about," Molly retorted, spitting a pit in his vicinity.

Pim picked up the pit and looked at it in the palm of his hand before he pushed it into his pocket. "Maybe we should work out a plan that doesn't mean chaining you to the tree."

"But what else can we do?" Molly said with some irritation.

Pim rocked back on his heels as if he was astride a magnificent horse, perhaps even a unicorn. Then he swung himself up onto the platform.

"We'll find a way to stop them, once we put our minds to it."

Molly shook her head. Her mind was already stretched. Pim ignored her and began to think. He took Molly's discarded fruit pit from his pocket and tapped it against the branch. It made a ticktock noise.

"You'll interrupt the vibrations," warned Molly.

Pim peered over the fence into the Grimshaws' bare yard. He glanced at the letter and then sat on the platform and dangled his legs over the edge.

"The way I figure it, you're in a bit of trouble, and vibrations aren't going to get you out. Your mother is a tree, or to put it another way, this tree is your mother, and in three days' time your neighbors are going to cut off her branches. We either work out how to stop them or we work out how to turn your mother back."

89

Molly was momentarily impressed. What Pim Wilder said had the cool, reasoned tones of something that might be true. Yet she wasn't sure she liked it. This was her trouble, not his. Who was he to suddenly sound knowledgeable? What would he know? He might know how to make a pulley system, but he didn't know one thing about potions or herbs or vibrations or anything.

Molly dug her heels down and wrapped her arms around the branch. She would stick to her original plan. *Her* plan. She shut one eye and leaned her ear against the branch.

"Shouldn't you be at school, Pim?" she said.

The tree rumbled. Indeed, it seemed to Molly that a deep, painful groan swelled up from its trunk and hummed down the branches. She lifted her head in surprise.

"Did you hear that?" she whispered.

"What?"

Molly frowned. If Pim hadn't heard it, then it must have been meant just for her. It was her mama sending a warning. Perhaps her mama didn't believe in Molly's plan to chain herself to the tree either. Molly wriggled uncomfortably. She let go of the branch. For a moment she said nothing and neither did Pim, though he did smile at the owl picture stuck on a twig.

Pim swung himself down. "Well, I'm going to school, then."

"Wait," Molly said. "We turn Mama back. We do it before Saturday, and if we don't, then I chain myself to the tree."

Pim smiled. "You're the boss," he said.

Molly rolled off her branch and somersaulted down.

"And you're really good at making pulleys. Thanks, on behalf of Maude especially, and for the buns too."

Pim cupped his hand to his mouth and sent two long hoots over the Grimshaws' fence, and then he picked up his bike. "The battle cry," he explained. "Are you coming to school? You want a lift? It might not be a cool double-seater, but it goes."

Yarrow

CHAPTER 15

BEST FRIENDS

Molly sat on the rack on the back of Pim's bike. It was much less comfortable than the yellow bike and she yelped when they went over the curb.

"Sorry," Pim said, "I warned you."

"You don't have to ride like a maniac, though."

"I do, actually, if you want to get there on time, and you should go in before me so nothing looks out of the ordinary. Otherwise, everyone at school will start wondering."

"Not just everyone at school, the authorities too," said Molly with a shudder as she thought of her chocolate balls crammed in the fridge. "And they'll take me to an orphanage and whip me if I'm bad."

"And you'll probably die of pneumonia too and be buried in a shallow grave and—"

"Not funny," grouched Molly.

But Molly's absence hadn't gone unnoticed. It turned out she was quite late, and when she entered the classroom, things were already under way.

Miss Todd threw her arms in the air. She was holding a pair of scissors in one hand. Her red hair was bundled in an extravagant bun as usual, and her dress, which was a bold lilac-and-purple floral, hugged her large, round body with the air of drama that Miss Todd liked.

"Molly, dear, I was just about to call your mother to find out if you were unwell too."

Ester Morhigg stood beside Miss Todd and stared at Molly.

"We're making get-well cards," Miss Todd explained, taking Molly protectively by the shoulders. "Have you been unwell?"

"No," said Molly. "My mama was unwell and I had to take care of her." She tried to keep her explanation as close to truthful as possible. Her mama thought that the truth was important, and somehow the things her mama thought mattered more now than they had before. Before, when her mama talked about things such as truth and kindness, Molly had never paid much attention.

Before Miss Todd could inquire further about her mama's health, and before Molly would have to entangle herself further in her small dance with the quiet untruth, Molly asked who they were making get-well cards for.

"Why, for Ellen Palmer! She's gravely ill. Would you like to make a card too?"

Molly gazed around the class to make sure this was true. Ellen was not there.

Miss Todd's words "gravely ill" boomed in Molly's head. What did they mean? Was Ellen, her best friend, lying on her bed with her eyes closed, deathly pale? Molly took a piece of colored paper and headed for a desk. And why had life suddenly steered so far off course? First her own mama and now Ellen, her best friend.

"Why is your hair so messy? Looks like a bird's nest," said Ester Morhigg. "Look at my card; I drew a horse. Ellen likes horses." She shoved her card in front of Molly's face. The horse was running across a field of green.

"I didn't know Ellen liked horses that much," Molly said softly. Perhaps she didn't know Ellen as well as she thought. Perhaps Ester Morhigg knew her better. Ellen was gravely ill and Molly hadn't even known. Her heart wobbled with an unfamiliar weight.

Molly stared at her blank card. She picked up her scissors. Her hand shook. A large tear rolled down her nose and dropped onto Ester's horse card. Miss Todd let out a gasp and flew to Molly's side. Molly stared in horror at the damp blob on the card. It was as if she had leaked. She wiped her eye and bit at her lip, determined no more would escape. She had promised herself never to cry, and she wasn't going to give in now.

"Molly, what's the matter? Is it your mum?" Miss Todd patted her back.

Molly nodded, and then she shook her head, and then she felt so confused she had to close her eyes and hold her breath and make everything stop. Then she stared at Miss Todd's big, wide eyes and took a deep breath. "I'm all right. I'm just tired, and I haven't got any lunch, and I'm worried for Ellen."

All these things were true, but perhaps the truest of all of this was that she was worried for her mama, and this was the one thing she couldn't say.

Miss Todd nodded. "You poor lamb. Come on. I'm going to take you to the cafeteria right now. Is your mother still in bed?"

Molly wished her mama was in bed. She just nodded, happy to be glided out of the classroom and to land in the cafeteria, where she ordered a sausage roll with sauce. After that, Molly felt she could face the rest of the day at school. But as soon as the bell rang, she ran all the way to the bridge, where she found Pim waiting for her, just as they had arranged. He was leaning over the rails, staring into the creek.

"I'm not going home right away," Molly said dramatically. "Ellen Palmer is gravely ill, so I have to go and visit her."

"Ellen Palmer? Gravely ill? Who said that?" Pim scoffed as he tossed his bag on his shoulder.

"Miss Todd."

"Miss Todd? But Miss Todd exaggerates everything. She thinks you're potentially dying if you cough." Pim threw a stone in the creek. It landed with an undramatic plop.

"Even so, I have to go. Ellen *is* my best friend. Will you come to my house later?" Molly still wanted Pim to help. She needed him. She had even felt happy to see him leaning there lazily on the bridge with his hands dangling and his long legs crossed.

Pim shrugged and nodded. "Okay. I'll see you in an hour." He turned to go and then he stopped. "If Ellen's your best friend, why didn't you tell her about your mum turning into a tree?"

Molly gaped. Pim wasn't afraid to say anything, even if it wasn't his business. How would he ever understand all the reasons she couldn't tell Ellen? He didn't understand Ellen like she did.

Molly frowned and lifted her nose proudly. "Ellen's quite sensitive. It would upset her. I didn't want her to worry about me." Molly turned away and she walked as fast as she could. It was true, Ellen would worry. But what she hadn't said was that Ellen would be terrified of something as unearthly as this. She might not even believe it. But Molly wasn't going to give Pim a chance to venture an opinion. She didn't want to hear it, whatever it was.

Snake

CHAPTER 16

SNAKEBITE

Ellen's mother had short brown hair, large shoulders, and sturdy shoes. She smiled easily and laughed in happy bursts, her voice always with a firm sound to it. But when she opened the door to Molly, she looked quite a different sort of woman. She wasn't as upright, and instead of sturdy shoes she wore slippers and blue pajama pants, and everything about her seemed crumpled. But she gathered herself and stood straight, and she burst out, "Oh, Molly, we're so worried." She drew Molly toward her and ushered her into the kitchen. Ellen's crumpled mother poured Molly a black-currant cordial, and she perched on a kitchen stool, seeming too tired to stand.

"May I see Ellen?" said Molly. "I haven't been at school, so I only just heard she was sick. What's wrong with her?"

"Well, that's the problem, Molly. No one knows exactly. It all started with the snakebite."

Molly gasped. Of all people, Ellen was the least likely person to get bitten by a snake. She refused to walk in long grass or to climb over woodpiles or even to swim sometimes in the creek, all because of the possibility of snakes. "Was it a brown?" Brown snakes were deadly, but so were tiger snakes.

"It was a brown," Ellen's mother said. "It was in the shower. We don't know how it got in there. But we took her to the hospital quickly enough. She should have recovered, but she hasn't. . . ."

Ellen's mum stopped and tilted her head, as if the weight of it all was leaning on her and she might topple over. She sighed and looked out the window at the garden with its brisk arrangement of lawn, fence, and tree.

"Now there are complications. Ellen is very weak and she can't seem to eat much. But I'm sure she will be happy you're here. She has been upset that she hasn't seen you."

99

Molly dropped her gaze. She was ashamed. What sort of best friend takes so long to visit? But she couldn't explain. She bit her lip to keep it all in.

Ellen's mother led Molly into the bedroom, which was dim, as the curtains were drawn. Ellen's mother changed as she entered the room. She spoke to Ellen in firm, reassuring tones, as if there was very little wrong. She sat at Ellen's side, told her Molly was there, and patted and kissed her before getting up to leave them alone.

Ellen lay on her back. Her hair was not in plaits but fell around her head as if it had spilled. She turned to see Molly. It seemed a great effort for her to do that, but her face brightened immediately.

"Hi, Ellen." Molly knelt down next to her.

"I'm pretty sick," said Ellen.

"I'm sorry I didn't come earlier."

Ellen struggled to sit up a bit.

"I can't believe you got bitten by a snake," said Molly. "Did it hurt a lot? It must have. But why are you still sick? Why can't you eat?"

Ellen blinked as if this rapid fire of questions was more than she had the energy or will to consider. Then she lay back to stare at the ceiling and sighed.

"Because I don't feel like it." She blinked again. "I'm too tired to eat or walk or anything."

"Well, you have to eat. Even if you don't want to. Just see it like math, something you have to do."

Ellen dismissed this wisdom with a slight frown. "Has your mama come back from Cuba yet?" Ellen said, and Molly was glad to see her face gather itself to express something, even if it was worry.

"Not yet. I didn't go back to school till today."

Ellen stared incomprehensibly at Molly. She closed her eyes for a moment. "Why didn't you want me to help? Did you think I would be too scared?"

"No, of course not. It was just . . . I was just managing fine on my own. And . . ." Molly stopped. She was going to say that since Ellen hadn't really taken the threat of the Grimshaws seriously, that had made her think Ellen wouldn't take any of it seriously, but Ellen was sick and she didn't need to be worried by Molly's feelings.

"And, Ellen, you're my best friend, and I can't get on with life till you're better. I'm going to make you something, and you have to promise me you will use it and get well."

"Okay." Ellen smiled, and looked for a moment

like her old self. Molly stood up. She squeezed Ellen's hand and left the room.

Molly was convinced that all Ellen needed was a little bit of courage, and surely she had that. Ellen could sing loudly and beautifully in front of anyone, while dancing too. That took something. Was it courage? Maybe confidence. Ellen had that. She had her own kind of strength.

Molly's mama made an oil, a green oil, that was meant to cure everything. She could give it to Ellen, as long as she could find the recipe and make it. Was the main ingredient the sap of spurge weed? As Molly walked home, she began to look out for it.

When she arrived at her house, she had a large bunch of spurge and her fingers were sticky with sap. Pim was waiting at the tree, sitting there with his back against the trunk.

"What's that for?" he called out.

"We have to make some green oil for Ellen. She really *is* gravely ill. Miss Todd wasn't exaggerating. She got a snakebite from a brown, and it has made her weak." Molly threw the pile of spurge at Pim's feet and washed her hands at the garden tap.

Pim picked a piece up and sniffed at it.

"Molly," he said. "How is everything in your life

so strange and urgent? And to do with plants and life and death?"

Molly frowned. She began to pluck rather violently at the spurge leaves. Strange was exactly what she didn't want her life to be. But if it was interesting, maybe strange wasn't so bad.

"I thought you wanted to help," she said.

"That's why I'm here, isn't it? I like it when strange stuff happens. Especially when it's big. When something's at stake."

He shrugged, and Molly stopped plucking quite so crossly at the spurge. She hadn't expected this. For one thing, Pim was a boy, and for another, he hardly knew her, or Ellen either. And he always seemed such a tough boy. She handed him a couple of stalks.

"You need to get the leaves off, and then we'll get the sap out," she said.

"But what about your mum? We're running out of time. Shouldn't we be working on that?"

Molly nodded. She hadn't forgotten, but picking the spurge had reminded her of times she used to gather herbs with her mama, and the stirring of these old feelings for plants had opened a part of her mind that she had been keeping closed. She had a feeling this was important; it was going to help her get closer to understanding the Mama tree. Perhaps it was like turning her mind over with a hoe and loosening it enough that seeds might begin to grow.

"Once this is done, we'll go inside and I'll show you Mama's notebooks. See if you can find any clues in them. They won't be what you expect, though."

Molly paused and screwed up her nose. "Thanks again for helping me, Pim. That pulley you built, well, it's so much nicer for me when it's dark to have Maudie up there with me. I hate the dark." What she meant to say was that more than anything it was having *him* there with her, even right then, that made all the difference. But it was easier to thank a boy for a thing than for a way of being. And Pim already seemed awkward, as he bent his head and mumbled something about it being okay.

They sat outside under the Mama tree, plucking at the spurge and squeezing the sap into a jar, while the tree bent its branches to shade them in the warm summer afternoon.

Mallow

CHAPTER 17

THE RED NOTEBOOK

Molly took Pim inside the house and handed him Mama's red notebook. It was a solemn occasion; Molly had only ever invited Ellen inside before. Pim stood with his back against the old woodstove in the middle of the room. He held the book reverently as he gazed around. Molly loved the house on late-summer afternoons, when the sun was low and came in with a deep golden light and made the dust motes sparkle. The scattered cushions and book-lined shelves now seemed welcoming, even inviting. Pim's gaze wandered over the shelves. He picked up a carved wooden elephant, examined it, and then placed it back on the shelf again.

"I tell you what, Molly. Even your house feels, well, it feels like a circus or a Gypsy tent. It's not like most people's houses. You're lucky."

"Lucky?" Molly laughed. She sat down at the desk where her mama worked. Behind her were shelves stacked with small, amber-colored bottles with white lids and labels such as LION'S FOOT, LOOSESTRIFE, and LOQUAT written in black felt pen. "I bet if you lived here, you'd wish you could live in a normal house, same as everyone else."

Pim snorted. "Why? Why would I want to be like everyone else? Boring. The world is full of people just like everyone else." He picked up a bottle. "Mallow! What's that for?"

"For softening, actually. When you're angry, you chew the root and meditate on your heart becoming warm, and you try to bring that warmth to the person you're angry at."

Molly was surprised she knew that. She was even more surprised she had told Pim, especially since feelings of the heart were not something she wanted to talk about with a boy. Perhaps she wanted to impress him with the things she knew that were different from what everyone else knew.

"You can eat mallow. Most people think it's a weed, but it's actually more nutritious than spinach." She tried to sound casual. "Is that why you hung the angel on the flagpole? To be different?"

Pim grinned. "Nah, I'm not trying to be different. Truth is, I like to find ways to make school more interesting. I have a whole book of photos of that angel in all sorts of different places."

"What do you want to learn at school?"

"Not football, that's for sure. And not multiplication tables. I want to know how stuff works. And how to make one thing become something else. Light, for instance, or sound. What does it feel like to fly? How does an albatross guide itself as it flies across the ocean? What's a star? It's not your kind of magic, but it's something."

Molly considered this. How could a boy not like football and like light and sound instead? These were not *things* that he liked; they were what colored the world, what gave it a certain feeling. She was about to reply that the magic was not hers but her mama's, but she stopped herself. She'd always hidden anything that belonged to her mama's world. But maybe having a feeling for plants was just like having a curiosity for how things work. Maybe Molly should start her own red notebook, take care of her knowledge. Knowledge was valuable, after all.

"Smell this. It's meadowsweet," she said, handing a bottle of tincture to Pim. "We might use it in the green oil. It gives the ability to change directions."

Pim whistled. "Right. So an herb can help you change directions? I'm not saying I don't believe, but I'd like to see for myself."

Pim bent his head to examine the red notebook. He drifted to the couch and sat down next to Claudine, who let out a large meow of protest. When Pim showed no sign of moving, Claudine leaped from the couch and circled Molly's leg sulkily. Molly, however, was busy pondering what Pim had said and she hardly noticed Claudine.

She hadn't ever imagined anyone would be interested in knowing about weeds. And it hadn't occurred to her that knowing this stuff could be something to be proud of.

Molly took the meadowsweet tincture and put it on the desk next to the jar of spurge weed sap. What else did her mama put in the green oil? Fat hen, three-cornered jack, curled dock, sow thistle, prickly lettuce, sticky weed, chickweed, yarrow. All these Molly could identify easily. Her mama used the leaves in pies or salads and boiled the crushed roots in syrup or made ointments by mixing boiled, chopped leaves in lanolin.

"Wow, this stuff is pretty out there! Listen to this," Pim interrupted her thoughts. "You know what it makes me think? Maybe it's not a potion that's going to turn your mama back into a person. Maybe it's something we have to do. A sort of ritual, or a dance?" Pim went on excitedly, "This page talks about merging with the plant. I think that's what happened: your mother merged with the tree. One thing became another. So, maybe you should try to merge with the tree too."

"We should dance with the tree?" Molly did a wonky pirouette.

Pim closed his eyes and put the notebook on his head. Molly laughed. He opened his eyes and grinned. Then he came toward her. "No," he said cautiously. "Not *we* dance with the tree. *You* dance. I think it's something you have to do."

Molly wasn't sure she would be able to create the right feeling on her own.

Pim headed toward the door. "I better get going. Mum will start getting worried."

"Are you coming back?" Molly's voice was thin, and it came out with a tremble. It wasn't that she was scared to stay there alone, because actually she felt safe sleeping in the boughs of the Mama tree, safer than anywhere else. It was more that she felt lonely, lonely in the way you feel when your life feels so very different from anyone else's. When Pim was there, she felt a little sense that he was sharing her problem. Even if it wasn't his mama and he couldn't feel what she felt, as least he knew about it. And once he left, she would be alone again.

"Well, I'll come back after school tomorrow."

"Okay," said Molly stiffly. She watched out the window as he grabbed his bike, swung a leg over the bar, and glided out of sight. And then she went and lay down next to Maude in the last golden beam of sunlight that spilled in through the window.

What she really wanted, Molly thought to herself, was to crawl into her mama's arms and tell her how very hard this was, and for her mama to tell her it would all be all right. She looked at her mama's empty bed and then she looked at hers, without its mattress. Both seemed so abandoned. Beneath hers a breeze caught at a folded piece of paper. It scuttled along the floor. Molly gasped. It was her last birthday letter. Her mama wrote her one every year. Molly had stuffed it under her mattress. And here it was escaping toward her. She ran over and scooped it up. It wanted her to read it, of course. Molly wouldn't have been surprised if the Mama tree had blown that little breeze in herself.

My dear Little Pump,
Here is my advice for my new ten-year-old.
You who are made of stars. Build a house inside
yourself. In it put that sweet little self of yours.
Be kind and gentle to it. When there is a storm,
don't fight, just surrender to it from inside your
little house. Let the wild weather take you where
it will. Welcome all the mysteries, uncertainties,
and doubts that life will throw at you with all the
wildness of a raging storm. And keep exploring.
You, my brave little love.

Molly battled back a surge of feelings. Life had certainly thrown a storm-sized mystery at her, and within it was every uncertainty and doubt that any raging storm could muster. It was as if her mama knew it. And if her mama was right, all Molly had to do was to hold on for the ride. She folded up the letter and tucked it into her pocket. She would put it with her other treasures in the tree. In her Mama tree.

Wild Oat

CHAPTER 18

DANCING

M olly lay in her bed of branches. Maude was beside her, curled up with her head on her paws.
Molly wrapped herself around Maude, and even
though Maude didn't particularly like being cuddled,
she put up with it.

"I know you don't like it, Maude, but that's why I
love you, because you let me do it anyway."

Maude raised her head and beat her tail briefly in
response, but then sank back down and seemed to fall
instantly back to sleep.

"Oh, Maudie," said Molly with a long sigh that
slid through the night and blended with the other

quiet, gentle noises of leaves whispering and faraway owls hooting and distant cars on some highway going somewhere. The world was never completely still and quiet, but the night had a special sort of hushed activity. Things rustled and seemed hidden within the blackness, and it was as if dreams bloomed like shadows and escaped from their moorings and grew in momentous, invisible ways.

Molly listened to the night. What should I do now? she wondered. Wondering was very different from thinking. Thinking always looked for answers. It was like folding the question up and putting it in the box it fitted into best. But wondering was like going for a walk without a destination in mind.

Could I dance around the tree like Pim said? Molly wondered. The tree was humming. Was her mama humming to her, calming her? Molly pressed her ear to a branch. The vibrations were smooth and syrupy. She curled herself around the branch. Then she sat on top of it and swung her legs. She was wide awake now. Around her Molly saw the garden: the black, silent forms of the trees and, as she climbed higher, the whole sloping valley of the town. The sky was a dark, glowing blue with wisps of clouds, a large white moon, and one shining star.

"Venus," whispered Molly. Her mama always

113

pointed it out. But tonight it was different, because it was Molly who had seen it, and because she had seen it and said its name, she felt she had introduced herself, and now she and Venus would forever know each other. It was like this with everything around her. It was as if she was seeing it all for the first time, seeing it with her very own self, taking the sense of it inside her. The black, shadowy tips of trees against the glow of light coming from the houses, the dark-forever-and-ever sky, the cluster of homes in the valley, where Molly imagined children snug in their beds, dogs flopped out tired on their rugs, someone rising from a piano, someone else sinking into a couch.

This cozy, golden light seeping out from windows made Molly feel she was watching the very great drama of inside and outside. The wild, dark sky and the star and moon and mountains and trees were all out of reach and beyond and wondrous and soaring like dreams. And the houses with their small lights were the steady, comforting bones of life, set snugly, one next to the other, together and connected like beads on a string. Yet inside wouldn't be inside without the wild, quiet roar of outside.

Somewhere out there, there was another child just like her, one who didn't live in a house, who didn't have a lamp on, who didn't have a mother or a father putting her to bed, and who didn't feel right at all. Out there in the wide world, there were hundreds of worries much, much worse than Molly's, maybe even thousands or millions of them. Molly's problem was a tiny dot in the night. And if you joined up all those dots, it would make the big, inexplicable shape of lives being lived.

Lives went in all ways. Life was a jagged dance of joys and sorrows, up and then down and sometimes in knots or jolts or dizzying rushes over or around again. And in Molly's town at that moment among all those houses that sat there in the valley, there was Ellen Palmer's house, where everything was always snug. But Molly's best friend was gravely ill in her own bed with the pink curtains and the dressing table and everything as nice as you could wish for.

Molly closed her eyes and wished for Ellen. She clung on tightly to her branch as if she and her mama were holding hands and both wishing for Ellen to get better. And it seemed that the branch clung back, just as it seemed that the sky swelled a little to fit that wish in, and the stars shone more with the feel of it.

"A million tiny stars," said Molly to the night, "and one more now." Molly smiled. This was exactly the strange sort of wisdom her mama would utter, and now Molly had said it herself. More than that, she had felt it.

Those stars swirled in her head and jiggled in her heart. She slid along her branch and made her way down the tree, swinging from branch to branch easily, nimble as a monkey. Perhaps it was magic, perhaps it was that she knew her mama wouldn't let her fall.

Imagine if you were never scared of falling, how much higher you might climb, she thought. Or, if you weren't afraid of being clumsy and awkward, how much more gracefully you might dance.

Molly jumped to the ground. The dark crept toward her, long black fingers of it. She leaned into the tree's trunk. The sound of her breath echoed back from the tree. She could break the dark's quiet. She could shake it all off her.

Molly stood so close to the tree the bark tickled her nose. She circled the trunk. She stomped, she shook. Her mind gave way to the night. She cried out. She flung her arms and shook her hands. She leaped and crouched and sprang as wide as she could and twisted and twirled till she was too tired to move anymore.

Then she stood very still and let her breath subside, but she watched the dark carefully. Had she frightened it away?

The night was still. The Mama tree was still, but Molly could feel something within it. It had a strange paleness, and it moved high in the branches. Molly rose on her tiptoes and angled her head to get a better look. Something lifted high above the tree and rose, spinning in the dark sky like a small spaceship. Then it fell, gliding down to Molly's feet.

It was her mama's sun hat, with the red ribbon dangling a little over the brim. She picked it up and clasped it to her chest. And then she climbed back up to her bed and lay down again.

A shriek pierced the dark. It was, no doubt, Prudence Grimshaw, alert as a hyena, attempting to scare a wallaby out of her garden. A chill crept along Molly's spine. She cuddled Maude and held on tight to the sun hat.

Comfrey

CHAPTER 19
THE WRONG WEED

The next morning Molly yanked Mama's sun hat out from beneath her and tied the red ribbon around her wrist. Because the Mama tree had sent the hat spinning down to her, like a trophy, Molly knew she was a step closer to wherever she needed to be.

"Well, Mama, I'm still here, and I'm not giving up either." She patted the branch reassuringly, and for a moment she felt as if she was the mother. She wasn't going to give any attention to her loneliness today; she wasn't even going to think about it. She was going to think about someone else's loneliness. Ellen Palmer's. She was going to do something about it too.

Molly got up quickly and picked herself some fruit from the Mama tree for breakfast. The flavors had changed. The white flesh now tasted like coconut and the green was like celery-and-potato soup. Then she swung herself down and hurried inside to feed Claudine.

It was time to find the rest of the weeds for the green oil. Molly took Maude, and they walked over the bridge to the woods where her mama had last collected herbs. Molly carried her mama's basket, and she wore the sun hat, which was slightly too big, and the brim made it hard for her to see ahead. She stomped along, looking down and crouching every now and then to pick some curled dock.

Molly and Maude walked for a while alongside the railway track, where the path was stony and the only weeds Molly found were plantain and some prickly lettuce, which she didn't pick, as she had forgotten to bring gloves.

Molly wished she could remember the exact recipe. She had a feeling there was nettle in it and comfrey, which both grew in their vegetable garden. And she was certain there was spurge and calendula and tansy. She needed strong herbs that could, for instance, grow on a parched, stony path. These would give the strength that Ellen needed.

Once home again, Molly set about making the green oil. She took down from the shelf some of the tinctures from her mama's collection, and the milky spurge sap that she and Pim had squeezed, drop by drop, into a jar. She boiled up the fresh weeds and mixed the strained water with the herb tinctures and some olive oil. She hoped that would do it.

She put the jar of sap with the bottled tinctures and read the names out loud to make sure they all sounded as if they belonged. She closed her eyes and tried to feel love; her mama said it was important. But all she felt was a strange tapping at her heart, as if someone was locked up in there and wanted to escape.

Molly opened her eyes and let out a short, loud, busy sort of sigh. It was hard to summon feelings exactly when you needed them.

She lifted the bottle of calendula tincture and poured it into a mixing bowl. She hardly noticed Claudine, who had been circling Molly's leg beneath the table and who now leaped onto the table, knocking over the jar of spurge sap. The sap spread in a useless white puddle on the table.

Molly looked at it in horror. Claudine sniffed it disparagingly, as if to say, "It's not even real milk." She leaped down again and sat with her tail curled in, looking elsewhere, as cats sometimes do when they think they might be in trouble.

"Well, Claudine, if you think this is going to make me get you some milk, you are very, very wrong, as now I think you are just a spoiled cat, and I am not in the mood at all for trying to find you some milk." Molly threw her arms up. "You've ruined my green oil. Ruined!" she added dramatically.

Molly pushed aside her mama's notebooks, which were smeared with spurge sap, and as she shook one dry, a piece of paper fell out. She picked it up and read it. It was in her mama's handwriting.

Uses for petty spurge, also known as milkweed, wartweed, radium weed: sap burns off sunspots, warts, corns, and some skin cancers. Active ingredient: ingenol mebutate. The sap is toxic and should not be used internally.

"Oh, wow," said Molly out loud. Claudine glanced

slyly back toward her. Molly had got it wrong. The sap from spurge was used for removing things, not for nourishing. Molly shuddered as she imagined what might have happened if Claudine hadn't knocked it over. She squatted next to Claudine, who turned her head away huffily.

Molly patted her under her chin, just where she liked it. "Okay, Claudine. I'm sorry for being mean. You were right. You even saved the day. And I will try to get you some milk."

It was some time before Molly set to work again on the green oil. First she began reading her mama's books about plants. But she knew she was avoiding the oil because she'd almost lost her nerve. And, even worse, she was waiting for Pim to show up. Molly didn't like to admit this to herself, because she didn't like to feel she could possibly be depending on Pim Wilder. She was the one who knew about plants, not Pim. It wasn't as if he would know what to do. And even if he did make suggestions, it wasn't his best friend who was ill, so he wouldn't put the right feeling into it.

And yet, Molly did like having someone to talk

things over with, and she liked it when Pim was there because he always had a way of seeing things that made her look at them from another side. He was so different from Ellen. Ellen was like a nice warm home: she was safe and sure and always the same. Pim was like a walk in the woods at dusk: full of darkness and brightness both at once, he was restless and un-fitting, pouncing on ideas and lifting them out of the dark. Pim's world was the mysterious world of owls, stars, animals, and earth. And Ellen's world was close by and welcoming, a place you could burrow into.

Where did Molly's world fit alongside these? Was she betraying Ellen if she became friends with Pim?

Her head spun. She went back to the green oil. She chopped and pummeled the weeds, her mind full of wonder and resolve. She had a job to do and some thoughts to think. It seemed that everything in her was expanding, straining to become large enough to hold all that at once, all the worlds, weeds, and won-der spinning within her.

And now it was already the afternoon. Molly would have to hurry if she wanted to make it to Ellen's and back again before dark.

But where was Pim? Molly stifled a pang of worry. Had he got tired of helping her? Had something else come along that was more interesting? It couldn't have; nothing could be more interesting. Perhaps he just didn't want to come anymore? What if this was true? Would she be able to do this all on her own? Molly felt torn. She wanted to help Ellen, but she wanted Pim to help her. Could she have both?

Right now she couldn't imagine life without either of them. But she had promised herself she would be strong today. Today was not a day for her to get stuck in her own fears. She would go to Ellen's now, and she would leave a note on the tree for Pim, just in case he did come.

Fat Hen

CHAPTER 20

SPAGHETTI

Ellen Palmer's mother was surprised to see Molly at the door again. Not only because she wasn't expecting a visit, but also because this time she noticed that Molly looked quite disheveled. Her hair stood out from her head, and she had slept in her dress, which was full of creases and covered in dirt and green, blotchy stains from the juices of the tree fruit. Molly clasped her mama's sun hat in one hand, and in the other a dark bottle with a white lid. Around her wrist was a red ribbon and she wore short boots with no socks. None of this Molly had taken any notice of. Her eyes were tired and hopeful and almost glittered with an unnatural wakefulness, so that she had the look of a worn-out traveler with an important message.

Molly was ushered into the kitchen, where Ellen's family sat eating spaghetti Bolognese. Ellen's father dabbed at his mouth with a napkin and said hello, and Ellen's younger brother, Jeremy, stared at her, with his fork pointing upward. There was Ellen's world, cozy and just right. Molly could have just sunk down and curled up there, if there wasn't an urgent task at hand.

Ellen's mother offered Molly some spaghetti.

Molly shook her head. "I have brought some special healing oil for Ellen. She has to rub it on her chest and on the soles of her feet and also where the snake bit her."

Ellen's mother looked unsure, Jeremy smirked, and Ellen's dad frowned at Jeremy.

Molly wrinkled her nose back at Jeremy before stepping toward Ellen's mother. "My mama has cured many ailments with this oil," Molly said. It was true that the green oil had cured lots of illnesses, but Molly didn't know if it had any effect on snakebites. She lifted her shoulders proudly and handed the bottle to Ellen's mother, who still looked a little startled and confused, but she took the bottle with gratitude.

"Thank you, Molly. Please thank your mother too. I have heard marvelous things about her cures." She glanced at her husband.

"I'm sure it won't do any harm," Ellen's father said with a small smile. Molly could tell it was hard for him to smile. There was a very somber tone to the whole family, as if they had turned gray and old.

"Would you like to take it in to Ellen? I'll see if she is awake." Ellen's mother's voice wavered and she looked away as she handed the bottle back to Molly.

Inside Ellen's room, a large floral armchair had been pulled up by the bed. Molly perched on the edge of it.

"Back again . . ." Ellen seemed grateful and a bit surprised.

"I told you I'd be back, remember? Here, Ellen, look what I have. This potion will make you better."

"A potion?" Ellen tried to sit up.

"Yes. Don't be scared," said Molly. "Mama knows about plants and how to make potions from them. She makes people better."

Ellen looked doubtful. She undid the bottle and sniffed at the oil. "Where do I rub it?"

"Here. And, Ellen, it's best if you sing while you do it."

"Sing? Sing what?"

"Doesn't matter what. Sing something cheerful and full of life. You're a great singer and it makes you feel good, so do it. Can I go and tell your mum to bring you some spaghetti?"

"Hang on a minute." Ellen propped herself up. "You never give me a chance to think. You always rush into everything."

Molly dropped her head; she was surprised. "Do I?"

"Yes, but sometimes your thoughts get to the finishing line before I've even started, and I get stuck not moving. You pull me forward. I'll eat some spaghetti; I don't want you getting sad too."

Molly grinned and stood up.

"But I don't know why you didn't tell me about your mother's potions. I would have loved to know about them," said Ellen.

"Maybe I was scared," Molly said. "Maybe everyone has something they're scared of. You are scared of snakes and crossing creeks on logs. But I'm scared that people won't like me because . . . well, because my family isn't like everyone else's. My mama eats scrambled tofu, my dad is lost in Cuba, my brothers are far away flying hot-air balloons." Molly still couldn't quite say that her mama had also accidentally turned herself into a tree.

Ellen frowned. Her lip quivered. And then she closed her eyes to think. "But, Molly, I don't think you're different. Or if I do, it's exactly what I like about you. Sometimes I feel that you think I'm not interesting. I thought you were bored with me. I thought that was why you didn't let me come to your house when your mother was away."

Molly's heart pitched about within her. She felt unsteady. Was that what was making Ellen sick? Her mama always claimed that bad feelings were bad for the body. Ellen thought Molly didn't find her interesting.

Ellen had felt as boring as Molly had felt weird. But none of the differences mattered. Or, they did matter; they mattered because they were important and wonderful. They were all part of a magnificent plan that made the world more interesting. Molly could like Ellen with her plaits and practicalities, as well as liking Pim with his owl sounds and curious taste for adventure. It was like being able to eat different meals. Molly should have given Ellen the chance to see her unusual ways, instead of always hiding them away.

If Ellen hadn't been so ill, Molly would have

jumped on the bed and given her a big hug and confessed that right now her mama was a tree. But that could all wait.

"Ellen, here's the deal. You stop being sad, and I'll stop trying to be just like everybody else. I like you just as you are, and you like me, peculiarities and all. Everyone has their own world: you, me, Pim Wilder, everyone. We're all like little stars, shining as hard as we can, with our own particular kind of light."

Ellen looked curiously at Molly. "Our own particular light," she echoed.

"Yeah."

"Little stars." Ellen's face broke into a mad sort of grin. She pulled herself up and reached out her arms to Molly, and Molly dived in for a hug.

And Molly felt the warmth of everything pressed and held between them.

Powerful Owl

CHAPTER 21
OWL HOOTS

Ellen's mother almost cried with relief when Molly asked for a bowl of spaghetti for Ellen. She rushed it in to Ellen straightaway and forgot to offer Molly some. Molly was alone in the kitchen, surrounded by the smells of spaghetti Bolognese, which traveled straight to her empty stomach. But, she thought, if she kept thinking all the way home about how hungry she was, her Mama tree would make some fruit that would just taste exactly like spaghetti. Not spaghetti Bolognese, as Molly's mama was a vegetarian, but spaghetti with tomato and olives.

This was what Molly thought about as she hurried home. She clambered down the side of the valley that led to the small black creek, now bloated with the croaking of frogs. Above it bugs buzzed and danced. Night colored the sky.

For a moment Molly wished she had told Ellen's mother her secret. It had pounded frantically inside her as if trying to burst out and land snug in the lap of Ellen Palmer's mother. Instead, here she was in the dusk, all alone, shouldering something bigger than her shoulders could carry.

From the other side of the valley there came a soft, insistent hooting.

"Is that you, Pim?" she called out.

Two more hoots sounded. Molly ran up the hill. Dilapidated sneakers and a khaki cap poked out from behind a bush. Pim had his hands cupped to his mouth and was making a whistling, hooting noise.

"What are you doing?" she said.

"Being a powerful owl. Did I convince you?"

"No. Well, almost," Molly admitted. "Did you get my note? Where were you today?" She was glad to see him.

"Busy. I had stuff to do."

Molly battled with a fleeting moment of jealousy. How could Pim have anything more important than their mission to turn her mama back? Molly started to climb the hill toward her house. She didn't care about Pim's owl sound at all.

"Hey, where are you going?"

"Home. I've only got tonight left. The Grimshaws are coming tomorrow with the chain saw," Molly said, just in case he had forgotten there was something more serious than owl sounds or other stuff to consider.

Pim caught up to her. "I know. I told my mum I was going to stay at a friend's place tonight. I'm sleeping in the tree with you."

Molly's cheeks reddened. He'd said "a friend's place"? She and Pim Wilder, friends? Yes, it was true. She and Pim had become friends.

As she pondered this, a large black car came powering toward them. They had to jump off the road to get out of its way, but not before Molly caught sight of Ernest Grimshaw at the wheel and Prudence Grimshaw, stiff as a peg, beside him.

"Did you see that?" Molly shivered. "It was the Grimshaws."

Pim watched the car as it sped away. He shrugged. "Driving like that, they are probably just compensating for their small minds. Come on, let's go before it gets dark."

Above them was the glowing sky. Before them the road home. Molly smiled to herself. Now that Pim was there, everything was thrilling again. Everything was possible. The Grimshaws were defeatable. They weren't as big as they thought they were.

Sometimes, she told herself, you can't figure things out, you just have to live them out.

Pim's Tree

CHAPTER 22

CONNECTIONS

As soon as they were back at Molly's garden, Molly and Pim climbed the Mama tree. The leaves rustled soothingly. The sky was dark and pink, and everything felt soft and full, as if the day's brightness had all been drunk and was now settling, sifting down, spreading.

Pim reached up and picked some fruit. Then he nodded at a rolled-up piece of paper that was lying on top of Molly's nest bed.

"Well, we can always go with plan B," he said.

"What's that?"

"Have a look. It's what I was working on yesterday.

I brought it here earlier and then found your note, so I went down to the creek to meet you."

Molly began to unroll the piece of paper. Pim hadn't forgotten their mission after all. She grinned and stood up, holding the paper against the trunk. It was a drawing of a tree, and around it were words that seemed to represent thoughts that had grown out of the tree.

It made Molly feel very serious. She felt she was getting closer. She grabbed the flashlight. "Come on, I think we need to get down to look at it properly," she said.

They unrolled the paper and laid it on the grass, pinning its corners down with stones. Maude sat on it. Molly called her off and squatted beside her to give her some love.

Pim shone the flashlight on it. The drawing lay before Molly like a strange, mystical map. Her heart leaped toward it.

What made it so entrancing? Was it that Pim had done it? Was it that he had done it for her? She read part of it again.

It seems sometimes to have wounds, which it grows around or over or despite them. (Like we do.)

Molly looked up at Pim. Did her mama have wounds too? Did she know that Molly was wishing

for a mother like Ellen Palmer's instead of her own?
Was she hurt? Was that why she wasn't coming back?
Molly's body twitched. She took in a sharp breath.
Pim gave a curious smile. Molly ignored it. Now that
her mama was gone, she wanted her back exactly as
she was. That's it, thought Molly.

As if Pim had heard her, he said, "I think that the
kind of magic we need is going to come from being
close to things, I mean trees, animals, earth, sky. We're
all made of dirt or flesh and blood or sap and air and
spirit and stuff. We are all sort of the same."

"So?"

"So we should be able to connect one to the other."

"But how does that change Mama back?" Molly felt desperate. What was her mama feeling inside that tree? Were her branches heavy? Was the sun hot on her leaves? Was she sad and worried and desperate too? Did she know it was only a matter of hours before her branches would be cut off? Molly couldn't let that happen. But she couldn't meld things together in her mind. Tree, sky, magic . . . Where was her mama in all of this?

Pim was shaking his head, as if something had lodged in it and he wanted to get it loose.

He began to pace.

"It's all about connection. Magic. Life. Forces of nature. We have to find a way to hook into the forces of nature to make that connection with her," he muttered, as if he was thinking out loud.

"I danced." Molly almost shouted this, and it came out unevenly, because she cut herself short, realizing it had been a private thing.

Was dancing a force of nature? Molly wasn't sure. Seals danced. Bees did too. And it had counted for something, because the hat had come to her. A connection had been made. "I danced with Mama," she said. There, it was out. "And afterward her hat flew off the tree and came to me."

Now it was Pim who gazed admiringly.

"You danced with her? Why didn't you tell me? That's amazing. You did it, then. You knew all along. That's why you're wearing that big, funny hat!"

Molly frowned and touched protectively at the hat's floppy brim. She spoke with some deliberation. "It wasn't that I knew it. It was more that I felt it."

"A feeling, not a knowing," Pim said. He began to pace again. And then his finger wiggled in the air, drawing something down from it. But before he could make any calculation, before he could say anything, Molly leaped up.

"Shhh." She held her hands still. "It feels . . . it feels . . ."

What did Molly feel? She needed quiet. She knew it was important and that it was more than Pim could work out, more than his wild thinking could uncover. But there was too much. She couldn't look at the drawing. She couldn't look at the Mama tree.

Molly knelt down on the grass again. Claudine appeared from beneath the lilac bush; she stood still and looked at Molly with a challenging stare, her eyes glowing in the dark. The garden seemed large and still and waiting: every tree listening with the tips of its leaves, every sprig of flower leaning toward her, expectantly. But was it waiting, or was it telling her what to do?

Molly put her hand on her heart and listened. Every current within her rushed toward it and swelled beneath it, wanting. . . .

"Every time I needed something, the Mama tree gave it to me," she said. That was it. From the very first vibration Molly felt when she'd needed to know, her mama was there. And when she had been scared of the dark, the tree had lit up and drawn her toward it. And when she had been tired, the branches had made themselves like arms to hold her. Yes, that was how it was.

It came to her now in a flood. She'd leaned into the tree and felt faint with hunger, and the tree had grown fruit. And when she'd threatened to chain herself to it, it had grumbled, to help her change her mind. And then, of course, there had been the dancing at night, the speak-to-me dance, the wild, true, force-of-nature dance that had released the hat to her, as if her mama had thrown it off to say, "Well done! Well done, my darling."

Pim was watching her. "It's true, Molly. It's wondrous and true, I'm sure."

Arnica

CHAPTER 23
YELLOW ROSES

Saturday arrived with the same bristling fervor as the Saturday before, when Molly's mama had accidentally drunk the acorn potion and turned into a tree. But instead of lying with her eyes shut against it all at the base of the tree, Molly slept soundly in the branches.

She was woken by Maude's loud and frantic yelps. She sat up, dazed. It had been quite a night, and she took a moment to reassemble everything in her mind. She looked over to Pim. He was stirring in the branches.

Molly yawned and climbed to her feet. Her dress

seemed to be standing up with her, in angles of creases and dirt. She tried to run her fingers through her hair, but it was too tangled. She grabbed the sun hat and pulled it on over the knots, and then lowered Maude down in the pulley system. Molly climbed along the branch toward Pim and pulled on his toe. Pim hardly had a moment to open his eyes before the sound of a loud roar hurtled through the air.

It was the chain saw. Ernest Grimshaw was warming it up. Pim and Molly stared at each other in horror.

Moments later Ernest and Prudence Grimshaw arrived in the garden, wearing matching canvas hats and army-green rubber boots. Ernest Grimshaw wrenched the chain saw in the air and gave it a threatening rev. His eyes rolled slowly around the garden, and his stomach bulged beneath a black collared shirt. He suddenly yanked at the hawthorn bush and pulled its branches sideways, as if looking for something suspicious hiding there.

Prudence Grimshaw stood, hard and gray as a steel spike, by Ernest Grimshaw's side. Her smile stretched her face taut as she gave a self-satisfied nod at Molly. "Where is your mother? We have come to cut down this blasted tree. And then we're going to shred it into wood chips. It makes a big mess. In the sky." She added this last bit about the sky with some satisfaction, as if it had only just occurred to her that this was the problem.

Molly backed herself up to the tree trunk, and Pim did too.

"You can't cut this tree, not one little bit of it," Molly growled.

Maude barked.

"We won't let you cut down the tree. We won't even let you touch the branches," added Pim.

Ernest Grimshaw jerked the chain saw upward and let it roar. He smirked.

"Where is your mother? Letting you run wild again, I see. What sort of a mother is she? Wretched woman. Well, I don't see how you can stop us." He revved the chain saw again.

Murder, thought Molly. That's what it would be.

Prudence Grimshaw now stepped forward, nose in the air. "If she had any sense at all, your mother would have removed the wretched branches. We told her to, and she ignored us. We don't like to be ignored, do we, Ernest?" she whined through her teeth.

"Mama doesn't want the tree cut down. It's a very special type of tree; in fact, the only one of its kind, and if you were nice people, you would see that! So, if you even try to cut it, we will call the police. And the

Tree Protection Society. They would be very angry if you cut it down," Molly shouted back.

Ernest Grimshaw's fat, sweating arms gripped the chain saw with determination.

Pim suddenly grabbed Molly's hand. "We won't budge until Molly's mum comes home, and if you lay a hand on us, we'll fight you. We'll draw blood if we have to."

Ernest Grimshaw's face ballooned, and Prudence Grimshaw began to quiver. Her eyes blinked rapidly.

Ernest blasted, "Worms! You are disgusting little worms! Mangy mongrels. Upstarts! Worms! I'll show you—"

Prudence Grimshaw let out one of her hyena screeches and flashed a warning glare at her thundering husband. "Wait." She glided forward, her fingers flexing like claws. "How dare you threaten us? How dare you? You will OBEY us. MOVE ASIDE!"

Pim let go of the tree and took a step toward Prudence Grimshaw. Molly wondered if he was about to tackle her.

"I've got bad news for you, Mrs. Grimshaw. We are not here to obey. We're here to think for ourselves."

"And you should treat us with respect," yelled Molly, anxious to get her word in.

Ernest Grimshaw pulled his wife out of the way.

He puffed up his chest and marched forward, as if into battle. "Brainless! Brainless fleas. That's all they are. *I'll* deal with them, Prudence."

Then, without really knowing why, Molly opened her mouth and screamed. And the scream pierced the air and rang out over the valley.

Ernest Grimshaw glared.

Then Pim screamed. And the two screams joined in the air and shook. Prudence Grimshaw's face crumpled at the sound.

Molly and Pim turned to face the tree and clung to it. They raised their faces, sending the scream up into the air.

Maude barked. Claudine paced.

Ernest Grimshaw's large, sweaty hands clamped on to Molly's shoulders. He yanked her away from the tree. But she jumped straight back to it. Then Ernest Grimshaw tackled Pim. "Blasted dimwit pups! You are in my way," he roared.

"Molly?" Another voice rang out across the garden.

Molly swiveled, but she still clung to the tree.

Ellen came running across the garden. She held a bunch of yellow roses, heads down, in her hand. Confusion clouded her eyes, but she still came, in a strange sort of breathless gallop.

"Who are you?" she said, staring at Ernest and Prudence Grimshaw. "Are you all right, Molly?"

Everything stopped for a moment, as if to make room for Ellen.

"Ellen, it's the Grimshaws. Come here and help me protect the tree. Hold it and don't let go," said Molly. "They want to cut it down."

Prudence Grimshaw pounced forward. She fixed Ellen with a menacing stare, and her voice came out in a snarl. "Little girl, we are here to uphold our legal rights to remove a tree that is overhanging our property, and if you don't want to get into trouble, I suggest you stand back."

"Don't bother trying to reason with them," roared Ernest Grimshaw, and he lurched forward again and began trying to tear Pim off the tree.

Ellen stared in horror. Then, shaking herself into action, she lifted her arm high and whacked Ernest Grimshaw over the head with the yellow roses.

Ernest Grimshaw turned on her, eyes blazing. "Hideous, hideous worm—"

Ellen didn't wait to hear what sort of worm she was. She hurled herself at the tree and held on, pale as a sheet. She sought out Molly's eyes, and together they opened their mouths and screamed.

Then came Ellen's mother, striding across the garden. She was strong again; her hair had its old upright composure, and she wore her boots.

"What on earth is going on here?" Ellen's mother looked accusingly at the Grimshaws. "It sounds like murder from the street. It's just as well I was waiting in the car."

Everyone looked at Molly. Even Pim. What would she say? Ellen's gentle, pleading face. Pim's dark eyes full of green and wonder. They flashed a warning, ever so quietly and quickly. Molly put her hands on the tree trunk. It felt warm.

"Mama went to Cuba," she said, "and the Grimshaws are trying to cut down her tree."

Ellen's mother frowned. "But she couldn't have left you all on your own and gone to Cuba? Surely? When will she be back? Who is your friend here? And what is going on with the tree?"

Ernest Grimshaw started up his chain saw. Molly wrapped her arms even tighter around the Mama tree.

"Move away," Ernest Grimshaw bellowed. "What sort of a woman goes to Cuba? The mother is mad. The family is deranged. The lot of them!"

Ellen's mother stood tall. Her shoulders rose. She glared at Ernest Grimshaw.

"If you lay a hand on Molly, or any other child here,

or that tree, I will call the police. I'll have you charged with assault. Now, back off."

Ernest Grimshaw looked as if he'd just received a blow. He staggered away from the tree and lowered the chain saw. His head quivered indignantly as he bit at his own rage.

Ellen Palmer's mother, who seemed to think it impolite to watch him, turned back to Molly. "Molly, I'm taking you home with us and we'll sort out whatever is going on. Maude can come too. And look how well Ellen is now, all thanks to you and your mother." She smiled and took Molly by the hand.

Molly let go of the tree. Her arms couldn't hold on anymore. There stood Ellen Palmer, sparkly shoes, a house full of muesli bars, grinning and well and welcoming. There was Ellen Palmer's mother, with her kind, strong arms, offering to take Molly to the house, the warm house made of bricks, with rooms and walls and windows and a television and a buttery cake in the oven. Everything she had always wanted. And there was her very own mama, her very own special, strange, ill-fitting mama, transformed into a very special, strange, ill-fitting tree.

Molly shook her head. She sank down to the base of the trunk and wrapped her arms around it. She wasn't afraid now. A great welling of feeling had erupted inside her, and it rushed up so forcefully that she pressed her hand to her chest, as if to quell it. Her body began to jerk and her eyes filled with tears.

Out came a sob, and then another. She wrapped her arms even tighter around the tree, and the sobs finally gushed out and tears streamed down her face, and her body gave way to it all. She wept as loudly and as fully and as wretchedly as anyone ever has. Her tears slid down the trunk and sank into the ground at the base of the tree.

"Mama," she sobbed. "Mama, I need you. I need *my* mama."

Rosemary

CHAPTER 24
ONE TINY BUD

The Mama tree began to shake.

The leaves whirled like tiny windmills. And the branches trembled.

Pim looked up and backed away from the trunk. Ernest Grimshaw's jaw dropped and so did his chain saw. Prudence Grimshaw swept to his side and drew him back, croaking, "Ernest, something bad is happening, something bad."

Ellen Palmer huddled close to her mother, who put her arm protectively around her daughter and frowned in disbelief. Molly continued to sob into the shaking tree. She seemed to have fallen into a trance.

Whatever was happening was happening because of her tears, and those tears needed to keep flowing to keep it happening.

The leaves whirled and the tree shook. And from the tip of the lowest branch, one tiny bud began to grow.

The branch creaked with the effort. It drooped and it trembled. And still the leaves whirled and still the tree shook. It sounded like a rocket preparing for takeoff, whirring faster and faster, as if it might at any moment burst from the ground and shoot upward. But one branch seemed to weigh it down, like an anchor. And at the very end of it, the tiny, pale-pink, fleshy bud grew larger and larger.

Soon, it was as big as a football. It began to hum and to glow with a strange shimmering light, as if each microscopic cell within it was alight and pulsing.

Prudence Grimshaw grimaced and recoiled, and from her throat came a gurgle of revulsion. She grabbed Ernest Grimshaw's sweaty sausage arm and tried to pull him back. But he shook her off, and he crept forward, examining the bud with his small, blinking eyes. Never in his life had he seen something that unsettled him as much. He picked up his chain saw, ready to attack the growing bud.

Pim stepped closer. The branch began to crack

and tear as the peculiar fruit continued to grow. The sound of whirling leaves and splitting branches became louder and more urgent. Ellen could hardly bear to look at the strange thing growing from the branch, but at the same time she couldn't tear her eyes away. Finally she cried out, "But what is it? What is it?"

Ellen's mother was completely still. She could barely speak. "It's . . . I don't know. But it's growing." That was all she could say for certain, and she did like to be certain. She squeezed Ellen's hand.

Molly raised her head. What was all the commotion? She had been so submerged in her own great storm of weeping that she hadn't noticed anything else till Ellen cried out.

Molly's face was tearstained and dirty; her eyes were red-rimmed; her hair stood out in knots. She said nothing. Her mouth was just a little bit open, and her eyes were wide as she caught sight of the astonished faces around her. But instead of sharing their alarm, she tilted her head as if the trance still had her, and stood up, twirling slowly on one foot, to face the thing they were all staring at.

It was now the size of a foal, kicking within its own skin, struggling and wriggling on its stalk. The strange, flickering light grew brighter, and the hum reached a high pitch, a boiling-kettle squeal. Molly

held out her arms as it grew even bigger. It seemed to be too heavy now for the stalk to hold it.

"Get back," Ernest Grimshaw shouted at Molly. How could he let a young girl get closer to the thing than he was? He started up his chain saw. "I'll get it," he yelled.

Whether Ernest Grimshaw really was going to cut it, no one will ever know. He was looking too afraid to go near the fruit, but, just in case, Pim dived at Ernest Grimshaw's rubber boots and brought the horrible man down in a thudding, cursing pile of pummeling arms and piglike grunts.

Ernest Grimshaw's legs flailed and thrust, and Pim held tight like a cowboy riding a bucking bronco.

The growing thing now shone like a small sun, casting a pulsing light into the whole garden. The tree winced and shivered and creaked above it. Molly thrust her hands toward the light.

Ellen gasped in horror. Wasn't Molly scared of it? Then Molly, still holding her hands to the light, began to sway and stomp and shake. Was she dancing? No one knew what she was doing, least of all Molly.

The light began to turn red, and the hum became higher in pitch as if something was gaining speed. And the more Molly twirled and leaped, the more it grew, the higher it hummed, and the brighter it shone.

It seemed to be building toward some sort of terrible explosion. The tree swayed and let out a thunderous crack. Ellen screamed and flung her hands over her ears. Prudence Grimshaw let out a shrill cry and clawed at Ernest Grimshaw, who was still grunting as he battled with Pim on the ground.

Molly began to crumple. She sank toward the ground as if her strength had been zapped.

And then, in one final jolt, the sky lit up as bright as a bolt of lightning. For just one second there was an eerie silence. No one could see anything. The sky was as white and bright as silver. And in that one dazzling moment of silence and brightness, the tree disappeared.

And out of the air fell Molly's mama.

She landed on her bottom on the grass. Then she stood up and frowned, rubbed at her bottom, and limped toward Molly, who had fallen in a lump on the grass. Maude dashed to her side, wagging her tail furiously.

"Well," Molly's mama said to the stunned crowd after she had gathered Molly up, "I'm not usually one to make an entrance, so please forgive me if I don't invite you all inside. I need a bath, and I think Molly does too."

Calendula

CHAPTER 25

PRUDENCE GRIMSHAW'S RUBBER BOOTS

Molly and her mama were a wild and disheveled pair. No one seemed to know what had happened or what was real and what was not.

Prudence Grimshaw took one look at them and immediately fainted. Ernest Grimshaw scrambled to his feet and backed away in horror. He took Prudence under the arms and dragged her, like a sack, out of the garden. In fact, the last view anyone had of the Grimshaws was Prudence Grimshaw's green rubber boots caught in the gate as Ernest tried to angle and jiggle her around it.

A few days later there was a FOR SALE sign on their house, and Ernest and Prudence Grimshaw never even returned to claim their turtle, which did reappear, only it had yellow cockatoo-feather wings stuck on it and it was raised on the flagpole.

But right now, Pim was thrilled by the great transformation that had happened before him. Like Molly, he had not taken fright at all. He picked up the chain saw and laughed. "Mr. Grimshaw forgot his weapon," he said. "Good thing he remembered his missus."

Ellen Palmer and her mother stood frozen and gaping; though after a minute, Ellen Palmer's mother remembered her manners and she closed her mouth and tried to smile. She kept looking at the spot where the tree had stood, and then she looked at Molly and her mama. She shook her head and walked gingerly toward them, holding out Ellen's bunch of yellow roses.

"Your tree just vanished . . . that whole huge tree . . . just went . . . into the air . . . ," she said. She stopped to make sure this was right, turning her head back to the spot and pointing. "And you appeared." She shook her head, knowing this wasn't possible. But it had happened; she had seen it with her own eyes.

Molly's mama began to speak, but Ellen's mother quickly intercepted. "There's no need to explain. We're relieved you're back, and we only came over to thank you and Molly for making Ellen well again. We're so very grateful."

Molly's mother smiled.

"It was Molly who helped Ellen, not me."

Molly looked up at her mama, and then at Ellen's mother, and then at Ellen. Everything was as it should be.

Ellen looked at Molly shyly. She opened her mouth to say something, but when Molly winked at her, she closed it and winked back.

Molly whispered, "Thank you for coming."

Ellen took her mother's hand and waved good-bye.

Only Pim remained. He turned to Molly, his face plastered with the broadest grin.

"Not exactly plan B, but brilliant anyway." He shook his head. "And you showed those brutes."

Molly grinned. Without Pim, her mama might well have ended up as a half-chopped tree, but her mind couldn't find the words to thank him properly. Instead, she scooped up her mama's sun hat, which had fallen to the ground exactly where the tree had once stood.

She frisbeed it to Pim. "Just so you don't wake up in the morning and think it was all in your imagination."

Pim laughed. "And, just so you know, you were right: that was the most interesting situation I've ever been involved in."

He tucked the hat under one long arm and threw the other arm indelicately into the air, as if throwing it away, in an awkward fit of jubilance.

As he walked toward the gate, Molly's mama called out, "Nice tackle, Pim. Thank you."

Pim saluted again, then jumped over the gate and rode off on his bike.

CHAPTER 26
PINHOLES OF LIGHT

Molly and her mama lay head to head on the seesaw and ate what was left of the chocolate balls. They both had clean, wet hair and scrubbed feet and were dressed in their most worn-in comfortable clothes. Maude lay happily at the foot of the seesaw, and Claudine sulked warily on the fence. The Gentleman crowed, even though it wasn't dawn. He must have sensed the evening's triumph and wanted to add his own note to it.

"She's cross with me for going away," said Molly's mama, who had given Claudine a tickle under

the chin to try to coax her down. "She does take things to heart."

Molly tried to imagine Claudine taking things to heart. Claudine never seemed to feel anything except from a distance, a place above them all, a clean, quiet, properly ordered place.

"But could you see, Mama?" asked Molly, sitting up and wondering if her mama had watched the whole drama.

"Well, I could feel you; I could feel quite a lot, actually. But it wasn't till I felt that you needed me that I found the energy to turn myself back."

She sat up and faced Molly on the seesaw. Molly squirmed and let out a long sigh. She wasn't sure she wanted to think about that, especially all those tears. She sensed her mama was working up to one of her talks. There she was, though, her real mama, exactly as she always was, still slightly messy and mismatched, a faded T-shirt, blue spotty skirt, and bare feet.

Her mama gazed at her intently: a little thought danced across her eyes. She smiled and, leaning forward, she put her hands on Molly's cheeks.

Here it comes, thought Molly.

"You know, Molly," she said. "There's a lot of

brave people out there in the world—fighting wars, risking their lives, making speeches—but there's another sort of courage. What you did took real courage. You showed your heart to everyone. You didn't care what anyone thought. If you hadn't had that courage, I would still be a tree. Now, that's a kind of magic you didn't know you had."

Her mama laughed. Her hands fell to her knees and she bounced the seesaw high.

Molly was still confused. "But, Mama, I didn't even know what I was doing."

Her mama slapped the seesaw triumphantly. "Exactly. You followed the wisdom of your heart. And you gave me the last bit of strength I needed."

"And, Mama, all the time I wanted to be just like Ellen, but now I'm glad I'm just like me. I can be Ellen's friend and Pim's friend, and I can be me."

Molly liked the way this felt. It was as if a great weight had fallen from her, and she bounced the seesaw as high as she could and felt she might float up into the evening sky. Her mama laughed too, and all the laughing tumbled out, careless and free, filling the air with its own sort of weather.

The evening was deep and low and quietly hovering on the edge of night. Cockatoos shrieked now and then in the pines. Everything seemed to brim and swell and to stand poised, ready to turn, or change. Molly felt ready. For what, she wasn't sure, but it seemed something had opened inside her.

There was a strange order of life, and she could feel it around them right now.

"Pim looks like an interesting boy," said her mama.

"Yes, he is. Come and I'll show you the picture he drew." Molly jumped off the seesaw and her mama followed. The drawing was still pinned to the ground with stones. They bent over it and read out the things Pim had written about trees, and Molly's mama nodded and seemed impressed that Pim was so very thoughtful about things that weren't quite certain and measurable.

Finally, Molly's mama groaned and unbent her knees and windmilled her arms in the air and said she had to walk, after having been a tree for so long. The worst thing about being a tree, she explained, was that you couldn't walk or run or leap, and these were all the things she was aching to do.

So they went with Maude, running and walking and leaping up the hill. They stood on the top of it in their favorite spot, next to the two gum trees, which always seemed like two old men, watching and sharing the occasional observation on the game. From there the town was a huddle of roofs and trees and streetlights, and on the other side of the hill lay the train tracks and the cricket oval, all bare and shorn like a bald spot.

Above them was the darkening sky and the large white moon. One bright star shone in the sky, but all the others, the millions of others, weren't there yet.

Molly thought about all the stars, getting ready to shine, waiting for the dark. They needed the dark. She slipped her hand into her mama's. The air was cool; the low sun shone through the long, dried summer grass and made it look as if their hill was covered in fine golden straws.

"Mama, even though it is the most terrible thing to have your mama turn into a tree, now that it's over, I think I am almost glad it happened."

"Why is that?" Molly's mama asked.

"Because now I have been the child of a tree. Imagine. But also, now I know how it feels to have a terrible problem, which is something nearly everyone knows some time or another."

Molly stood tall and she imagined herself for a moment on a horse, looking down at the world, ready to save it, ready to let her heart pound, ready to shine out in whatever darkness came at her.

"But no one can do anything good without a little bit of help," she went on, thinking mostly of Pim. And Ellen. Ellen had attacked Mr. Grim-  shaw with a bunch of roses. Molly laughed to herself. She was looking forward to going back to school with her two friends. Pim would keep things interesting, and Ellen would keep things real.

"You know what?" Molly said to her mama. "I'm starting my own notebook on plants, just in case you go disappearing again, or I do. There's stuff I'm going to want to know."

As they walked back, the stars began to break through, like shining pinholes of light in the dark above them, but Molly was too busy thinking about Pim and Ellen to notice the millions of tiny stars.

Molly's Notebook

Amaranth

Mama collects amaranth whenever she sees it growing. It has another name, which I like better: love-lies-bleeding. Sounds like a poem about lost love. But it's only a very nutritious weed. Mama steams it and serves it with olive oil and lemon juice for dinner, which is okay, but the Aztecs used to mix the seeds with cactus juice, honey, and even sometimes human blood and then offer it to the gods. Women used to use the red flowers to make rouge for their cheeks and dance around the fire.

Pomegranate

Pomegranates are not my favorite fruit. If I had a choice, I would prefer a mango. According to one tradition, each pomegranate contains 613 seeds, the exact number of good deeds a person should do in their life.

The Gentleman

Why does the Gentleman shout cock-a-doodle-doo at dawn? Apparently because he is a male and wants to let any other roosters know that if they try anything, like taking one of his hens or coming into his coop, he is up for a fight. In this way he is a bit like Ernest Grimshaw. It's a shame they didn't get to know each other.

Castor Oil Plant

I have drawn Prudence Grimshaw as a castor oil plant because it is a thin plant like she is. If you have ever tasted castor oil, you will never want to do it again, and if you have had anything to do with Prudence Grimshaw, you will probably never want to again. However, castor oil is very good for repelling moles from your garden, if you happen to have moles in your garden. If you are old, rub it on your wrinkles. Apparently, it works wonders.

Mandrake

I have drawn Ernest Grimshaw as a mandrake because mandrake is bulbous and dark and menacing. According to legend, when the mandrake root is dug up, it screams and kills all who hear it. And here is an old and nasty magic recipe.

Take a mandrake root out of the ground during a full moon. Cut off the ends of the root and bury it at night in a churchyard in a dead man's grave. For thirty days, water it with cow's milk in which three bats have been drowned. When the thirty-first day arrives, take out the root in the middle of the night and dry it in an oven heated with branches of verbena, then carry it with you everywhere to work your magic.

Acorn

I love acorns. I have always loved them. Because they come from oak trees and because they wear hats. No other seeds that I know of wear hats. People used to keep acorns in their pockets for good luck, for a long life, and to ward off loneliness. It is said that an acorn on your windowsill will prevent lightning strikes. Ellen and I play this game of fortune-telling. You can try it too. Take some acorn hats. Name one for you and one for your sweetheart, if you have one (which we don't, but we make up names just in case). Float them in a bucket of water. If they float together, it all looks good for your future, but if they drift apart, well . . . it may not last.

Borage

 Borage is an herb of gladness. Watch how the bees love it. Plus, it has merry little blue flowers, which I eat. If Ellen was a plant, she would be borage, because the flowers almost sing. It is said that if you steep borage in wine, it will drive away all sadness, but that may depend on how deep the sadness lies.

Lemon Balm Tea

When you suffer a shock—if your mama turns into a tree, for example—have a cup of lemon balm tea. You can mix it with licorice and ginger. Lemon balm is also good for your immune system. So if you get a cold, drink it up.

Lavender

Lavender and I get along quite well. I like its color and its smell. Last summer I picked it and mixed it with rice to make scented eye pillows. In ancient times, washerwomen, called lavenders, dried clothes by spreading them on lavender bushes. Great idea. I intend to dry all my clothes this way and waft lavender wherever I go. Lavender repels insects and soothes bites. (Try rubbing the oil on your mosquito bites.)

Sow Thistle

Sow thistle is a very common weed. According to medieval legend, cows like to eat it to help milk production. Aborigines were very fond of it, as were hungry explorers, which is what I may end up becoming. So it's a useful plant to know, wherever you are in the world, just in case you are hungry and have run out of chocolate-and-cashew balls.

Birdsong

Birds here aren't the sweetest singers. They prefer to screech loudly. It's annoying sometimes, especially the cockatoos, because they wake you up with their screaming. It's because they are defending their food from other birds. Many plants are bird-pollinated: banksias, grevilleas, bottlebrushes, grass trees, paperbarks, hakeas, and hundreds of eucalypts. Lots of feuds at the flowers mean that pollen-dusted birds are forever coming and going. Magpies are especially aggressive.

Chamomile

The word "chamomile" comes from a Greek word that means "ground apple." Chamomile is supposed to have a magical ability to attract money. Gamblers used to wash their hands in chamomile tea before they played cards or threw the dice. I think it's probably more often used to make a tea that has a soothing and calming effect on people who are too stirred up. Ernest Grimshaw could have done with some. It's best to steep the chamomile flowers for ten minutes before drinking.

Apple Tree

There is a legend of a man in America, Johnny Appleseed, whose dream was to plant apple trees all over the land so that no one would go hungry. He walked barefoot, slept outdoors, kept apple seeds in his pocket, and wore a tin hat, which he also cooked in. Think of him next time you have an apple. I do. I try to keep apple seeds in my pocket too. Some say that if you eat them, they will protect you from illness.

Wishing Tree

All over the world there are customs of hanging things (wreaths, ribbons, rags, etc.) on trees as a way of making a connection between people and trees. Every year Mama and I write a wish and tie it to the mulberry tree. It's our own personal wishing tree. Pim also has a wishing tree. His is a mountain ash.

Yarrow

Now we need to talk about herbs for courage. Yarrow is used for the wounded warrior and wounded healer as well as people who are struggling with overwhelming problems, like I was when Mama turned herself into a tree. I like to see myself as a warrior and a healer all at once. Best to be brave and wise; otherwise, courage can become just foolish and you end up being a show-off.

Snake

You can't rely on herbal remedies for snakebites, though I have read that the soaked bark of acacia or blackwood can be used to bathe the wound. Put a firm pressure bandage over the bite and then lie down and stay still while someone else calls the ambulance. But, even better, try not to get bitten in the first place. Sing out loud and stomp when walking in long grass on sunny days. It's more enjoyable too.

Mallow

Mallow is an often-overlooked weed. The ancient Romans considered it a delicacy. The Roman poet Horace wrote, "I graze on olives, chicory and simple mallow." He must have been hungry if that is all he ate. I hope he got some bread and jam as well. We eat mallow leaves raw in salad or cook them like spinach in a pie with cheese. Herbalists use it for sore throats. It's also good for soothing spider bites, bee stings, and burns.

Wild Oat

Like a long grass, wild and heartening, swaying in the wind.

Eat your porridge. Oats are good for you. And good fuel for the day ahead and, most of all, for the adventures that lie waiting for you. . . .

Comfrey

Comfrey was once also called knitbone, bruisewort, and boneset. It was used by ancient Greek doctors like Herodotus, Dioscorides, and Galen because of its ability to speed the healing of broken bones. Try placing a comfrey leaf in your suitcase to make sure it isn't stolen. Or if you are a more practical type, put it in your compost and it will help break it down.

Fat Hen

You can sneak fat hen into any spinach pie and no one will know the difference. And it's much more nutritious than spinach and has been eaten since prehistoric times. (Fat hen seeds were found in the stomach of the preserved man found in a Danish peat bog.) Fat hen can grow almost anywhere, even out of cow poo, which is why it has the nicknames dungweed and muckweed.

Powerful Owl

Powerful owls eat ringtail possums and roosting birds and sometimes a passing rabbit. They catch them with their feet. I would not like to be a small mammal passing beneath an owl. The thing I like about powerful owls is that they mate for thirty years. I am not sure if love comes into this pact or not, but it is nice to imagine it does. It makes up a bit for all the poor possums.

Pim's Tree

It takes the weather and makes food of it. It swallows the sun and rain, drags them inside, turns them into growth.

Tree stands through our whole lives. It holds the passing of time in the widening of its trunk, the lengthening of its branches.

It seems sometimes to have wounds, which it grows around or over or despite. (Like we do.)

It seems patient, old. True. Constant.

Arnica

I drew Pim as arnica because arnica makes a good salve for bumps, bruises, and sprains. Mix it with witch hazel and comfrey. I think arnica has a quiet but striking sort of grandeur too, and not in a usual way either.

Rosemary

It was believed that if you placed rosemary under your pillow, it would prevent nightmares, and if you planted it in the garden, it would keep witches away from your home. If rosemary grew in the garden, it meant the woman of the house was in charge. Men were annoyed about this and some were known to pull out all the rosemary plants to show they ruled. I bet there is no rosemary growing at the Grimshaws'. Rosemary is warming and it helps you concentrate and solve problems. If combined with borage, it makes a great tonic to give courage. Potatoes are so much better with rosemary. Eat it with your potatoes and go out to battle.

Calendula

At the end of the day, the end of the battle, the end of the journey, what we all need is a good bath. Calendula is a good herb to throw in your bath. It's soothing and healing. Mix it with sage, lavender, lemon balm, yarrow, basil, fennel, and chamomile. Close your eyes, soak it up, and be glad for everything you have.

Stars

When people look at stars, they often search for meaning. Stars encourage it. Because they shine mysteriously and brilliantly.

Astrology began when people made attempts to predict seasonal changes and weather patterns using the stars in the sky. Then they began to use them to forecast disaster and war. I'm pretty sure at some stage most people stopped believing in the stars, but I think it's best to throw your dreams into the night sky and then follow them anyway.

Acknowledgments

I would like to acknowledge the wonderful work of my editor, Jane Pearson. Thank you!